WITCH FOR THE WOLF

A NOVEL BY

ANNABELLE WINTERS

Books by Annabelle Winters

The CURVES FOR SHEIKHS Series

The CURVES FOR SHIFTERS Series

WITCH FOR THE WOLF

A NOVEL BY

ANNABELLE WINTERS

2019
RAINSHINE BOOKS
USA

COPYRIGHT NOTICE

WITCH FOR THE WOLF

1

The witch Magda folded her arms across her slight chest and narrowed her eyes at the two-year-old twins. They stared right back at her, unafraid, unflinching. They weren't scared. They were dragons. Years from their first transformation, yes. But still dragons.

"That's all right, little ones," she said with a tight smile that drained the color from her lips. "You have nothing to be afraid of. I do not eat children. I am not that kind of witch." She shrugged, winking at the wide-eyed children of the dragon and the bear. "But your grandpa . . . now *he* might want to eat you two for breakfast!"

Magda giggled, a nervousness underlying her laughter as she slowly circled the room, her small feet making no sound on the cold sandstone floor. They were in a gigantic black-marble mansion built on a small oasis not far from the Syrian border. Technically they were in Iraq, but this part of the desert was so vast and open that borders meant nothing and a man could claim the land as his own without anyone batting an eyelid. And that was just what Murad had done decades earlier, slowly building mansions, castles, and palaces in strategic locations across his claimed kingdom—a barren kingdom of sand and rock, no life other than a few groves of desert palms surrounding the scattered oases.

That's when Magda had run into the older dragon, a man torn in two by his inability to control his beast. The hoarding instincts of the dragon had served him well—indeed, Murad had amassed great wealth and swaths of land over the centuries. But the rage of his dragon was fearsome, uncontrollable, too dangerous for Murad to even venture close to civilization. The man had recognized that he had the ability to destroy the world, and the only thing that had kept him from doing so was the realization that the dragon would lose his carefully hoarded wealth and riches if he destroyed the world!

It was comical, really, Magda thought as she turned back to Murad's gurgling grandchildren, the twin children of Adam and Ash, a boy and a girl, each of them watching her with those blazing eyes: a combination of the green, gold, and brown of their parents.

Yes, it is comical, Magda thought as she continued to pace the room, waiting to make her next move, her anxiety rising. Murad was a caricature of a dragon when I met him—a deadly caricature but still a joke. It took my ambition to show him what he could achieve if his power were channeled, if his dragon was brought under his control. Under *my* control. But he feared his own dragon too much—*hated* his dragon even! He wanted me to *kill* his dragon with my magic!

"Can you imagine?" she whispered to the children, shaking her head and smiling. "Grandpa wanted to kill the part of himself that was most powerful! It was only when I assured him I could suppress his Change with my magic that he agreed to join with me. And look where we are now! Building an army! On a path to rebuild the world from its own ashes! A world where children like you can spread your wings freely!"

Magda hugged her bony shoulders and then stretched her arms out wide, her blood-red cloak flapping like wings in the warm desert breeze blowing through the large, unfurnished room. But Magda didn't have wings. She didn't fly. Not like dragons could, at least.

"If only . . ." she whispered to the children as they stared at her, still innocent and unafraid even though they'd been separated from their parents. Magda cocked her head as she once again marveled at how calm and collected these children were. Did they not feel fear? Was she not a fearsome creature of darkness and evil?

But she couldn't even finish the sentence she'd begun. She could barely finish her own thought! With a shake of her head she lowered her arms and straightened out her gown, patting it down carefully around her tiny waist and slim buttocks. She strolled in front of the floor-standing mirror, one of the few items of furniture she'd had put in this mansion. Indeed, Magda loved mirrors. She loved to look at herself. Slim. Sleek. Smooth. It reminded her of what she'd felt as a child when she was only just discovering what she was, what she was capable of being, what she was destined to be.

"It was a different kind of power I had back then," she whispered to the children, admiring herself in profile as she nodded. "A different kind of magic. That was taken away from me, but I gained something else in the bargain. Now I can do anything. Be anyone." She turned her head to the silent children, who still seemed inexplicably calm. "You want to see the real me? Yes? Promise you won't tell anyone?"

The twins both grinned at the same time, each of them saying something that sounded like "Yes!" Magda grinned back, showing her gleaming white teeth that were still sharp and pointy, like it was the one thing that hadn't changed about her when she'd lost that other kind of magic, that other part of who she was.

"All right," she whispered. "But don't tell anyone, you hear? They'll laugh at me. It's hard to be a fearsome witch when you're all round and cuddly. Hard angles work much better on a dark witch than a double-chin and a big ass."

Magda turned to the open balcony and sniffed the air. Caleb wasn't close. It would be another day before he arrived. She was safe. No one would see her like this. No one would see her true self.

With a trembling sigh Magda released herself from the magic that enveloped her night and day, a simple but powerful spell that she'd learned years ago. It took a moment for the spell to wear off, and Magda closed her eyes as she felt her body change, slowly regaining its natural shape, a shape she'd always hated.

When she opened her eyes she could see that the children were transfixed. They were wide-eyed, both of them smiling in awe as if they were watching a magical cartoon. Magda smiled back, feeling her filled-out cheeks move as she finally turned back to that mirror and gazed upon her reflection.

"Mirror mirror on the wall," she whispered to the short, dark-haired woman staring back at her: a woman with a round face, wide hips, thick legs, and boobs and buttocks that pushed her robe to its limits. "Who's the fattest witch of them all?"

You are, she said to herself as she stared at the reflection and smiled. You are, Magda!

"What?" she said to the kids, twirling her fat ass as she felt a strange relief pass through her, as if the magic she'd been using to change her appearance had been straining her from the inside, twisting her in a way that changed more than just her looks. "Why do you look so surprised, little ones? What's the point of being a witch if you can't use your magic to look thin? Am I right?"

She laughed out loud as she paraded through the room, once again feeling an odd sense of freedom when she felt her boobs jiggle, her ass shudder, her thighs tremble. What was that feeling, she wondered as an image of Caleb suddenly flickered into her mind's eye. Caleb the man. Caleb the warrior. Caleb the silent, solitary wolf-Shifter who'd fallen under her spell in a way she didn't think was possible. It wasn't easy to bring a Shifter under a spell, she knew. With humans it was easy. With animals it was simple. But with Shifters . . . yes, with Shifters it got complicated. You needed a way into their minds, into their souls, into their . . . hearts?

Magda blinked as she felt her heart flutter, those images of Caleb ripping through her imagination in a way that made her uncomfortable, made her uneasy, made her . . .

"No!" she muttered out loud as she felt the warmth rush through her curves. A feeling that she didn't think was possible for her to feel. She closed her eyes tight, whispering the words of her spell as she tried to force the images of Caleb out of her mind—images of his lean, hard, soldier's body, every muscle chiseled to perfection, tattoos covering his broad chest and thick arms, a back rippled with muscles so tight they looked like a pit of intertwined snakes, those high cheekbones, eyes blue like the ocean . . .

Suddenly Magda's eyes flashed blood red, and then the spell washed through her again, pushing away the warmth as her body once again shriveled down to the wire-thin frame of the witch inside, the witch she was, dark and dangerous, powerful and poisonous. This was who she was, she reminded herself as she felt the coldness of her dark magic roll through her, her bony fingers clenching like claws. That other woman was dead. That rosy-cheeked girl she'd once been was just a memory. They'd killed a part of her when she was too young and weak to resist, but in doing so they'd given this other part of her new life. This was who she was now, and this was her destiny.

Yes, *this* is my destiny, she thought as she glided towards the balcony and surveyed the barren desert. She smiled as she imagined the world stretched out before her, a world remade in her own image, where the guilty paid for their sins. *This* is my destiny, my fate, my meant-to-be. Even if the legend of fated mates is true, it cannot be true for me. Not anymore. My path was altered when I was a child, and this is now my fate.

This, not him.

Not him.

Never him.

2

"**Y**ou!" said Murad, scowling down from his gold-plated, jewel-studded throne on a raised platform of shining white marble. "Why are you here without your handler, Wolf?"

Caleb took a long, slow breath, his eyes narrowing as he looked up at the self-proclaimed Sheikh Murad sitting on a throne like he was actually a king of more than just desert that no one gave a shit about. He felt his snout twist into a scornful grin as he shook his head. This was Adam Drake's father, he reminded himself as he thought back to his time with Adam and Bart. The memories of that time were fleeting, hard to access, buried somehow. He could feel them inside, but he couldn't quite access them fully. It was like part of his soul was covered in a blanket, locked behind a door, held back by a power he couldn't quite understand.

He was in wolf form, even though he had the power to Change back and forth at will now. Magda the witch had somehow given him that power—or at least awakened that power in him. Still, he liked to stay in wolf form when in Murad's presence. He sensed it made the Sheikh uneasy, and Caleb liked to make the man uneasy. He'd never enjoyed taking orders from anyone, being a servant to anyone, a slave, a goddamn lap-dog! Hell, that was why he'd have never made it in the military, right? He was a lone wolf. A solitary soldier. Alone then. Alone now. Alone forever.

"I have a message for you, Murad," growled Caleb, his eyes glowing in a way that he knew was the witch's power flowing through him.

"*Sheikh* Murad," said the tall, bearded man sharply, standing up from his throne and staring down at the wolf like he expected Caleb to cower. "You will call me Sheikh!"

"Sheikh Drake?" said Caleb, grinning as he felt a rush of delight from how easy it was to rile up this asshole. "Got a nice ring to it. Sheikh Drake! Sheikh Drake! Shake a drake! Shake and bake!"

Murad's eyes flashed gold, his black robe shining with Magda's magic. Caleb went silent as he reminded himself that this man was a dragon inside, a bundle of coiled-up rage. Caleb knew what it was like to go against a dragon—he and Adam had gone at it a few times back in the day when they were first put together in that three-person crew, all of them going at each other, testing each other's strength like men did, like animals did. Caleb had understood the dragon's strength when he'd seen Adam Change, seen the dragon overpower even Bart the Bear. He grinned as he thought back to the time he'd tried to get between Bart and Adam when it looked like their horsing around was going to get someone hurt if not killed. One swipe from the dragon's tail and Caleb had been sent flying a hundred feet away! The guys had laughed their asses off that day! The Flying Squirrel, they'd called him. Shit, he'd been so pissed then! But now . . . now somehow the memory made him glow warm inside.

"The witch has your grandchildren," he said, reminding himself why he was here. Magda had sent him here, just like she'd sent him to kidnap Adam's children after drawing the dragon away from his lair. Magda was in control of him, but yet it didn't bother him as much as he thought it might. He enjoyed being around her. It gave him a strange energy that he sensed was not just magic—not *that* kind of magic anyway.

Murad cocked his head like a bird and stared down at Caleb. "My . . . grandchildren? Adam's children?" He blinked, drawing a slow, rasping breath as he rubbed his beard and began to pace. "The witch got to them?"

"Technically I got to them," said Caleb sharply. "And you're welcome, Sheikh Drake."

"I did not thank you, Wolf," said Murad. "A slave does not get thanked by his master. Remember that." The Sheikh glanced towards the open balcony, his anxiety clearly rising as Caleb watched with glee. The old man was scared, wasn't he. Scared that his son was going to fly in here, wings spread wide, maws open all the way, fire and vengeance screaming in with the hot desert wind.

Again the Sheikh's robe glowed with the dark magic holding back his dragon, and Caleb lost his grin and slowly began to back away. He understood why Magda had taken Adam's children. She wanted Murad to unleash his dragon—unleash it and gain control over it: Something he'd never been able to do, perhaps never*wanted* to do.

"Where are they?" Murad asked, taking deep gulping breaths as he pulled at his beard.

"Far from here," said Caleb. "Don't worry, Sheikh Drake. Adam isn't going to come flying in here. Not just yet, at least."

Murad snorted. "But he will come for his children. He did it once, and he will do it again. What does the witch expect to accomplish? She cannot control Adam with her magic. He will find her, and he will swallow her whole. I doubt the monster will even bother to crunch her bones when he eats her."

Caleb's neck-hairs stood up straight at the thought of Adam roaring in and attacking Magda, those powerful jaws of the dragon crushing her body. For a moment he wanted to turn and run back to her, stand before her so he could face Adam, so he could protect the witch, protect his . . .

Caleb frowned as he stopped himself from completing the thought. It was a thought that had come to him before, was coming to him more and more, especially when he was around Magda, when he could smell her scent, smell the woman in her. Sometimes her scent made him dizzy, whipping his senses into confusion, making him think that the witch was a facade, an illusion, that there was something hiding behind that thin, pale face, those dark, dead eyes. Something alive. Something warm. Something wonderful.

Something his.

"Kill them," came Murad's voice through Caleb's swirling mind.

"What?" said Caleb, a chill going through him when he saw the gold flash in Murad's eyes.

"You heard me," said the Sheikh, turning away from Caleb. "The children are of no use to me. They are no more than a tracking device for Adam and his dragon. You might as well send him directions to my location. Kill them and be done with it." He turned his head halfway and shrugged. "You can eat them if you like, Wolf. That's what your kind does, right? Go on. You have my permission. Shoo, little doggy. Off to your mistress."

3

Caleb resisted the urge to leap at the Sheikh's throat and rip out his voicebox. It took some effort, and Caleb was surprised at how fast his own anger had risen. It wasn't so much the condescending way in which the Sheikh spoke to him—hell, Caleb didn't get affected by assholes throwing insults at him. It was another instinct that fired to life at the command to kill Adam's kids. A protective instinct, fierce and undeniable. An instinct that Caleb knew would never let him hurt those kids. Those kids were Adam's flesh and blood. The offspring of his Alpha. They were family. Part of his crew. Part of his pack. He'd die before he let anything happen to them.

The realization sent bolts of electricity through the wolf's body, and he broke into a dead run as he left the Sheikh's palace. He wasn't sure where he was running to. He just knew he needed to run. There were instincts that were coming to life in him—feelings that had been buried so long he assumed they were dead. It upset him. It messed with the idea of what he thought he was, what he thought he was meant to be, what he thought was his fate.

"No!" he howled as he galloped into the open desert. "I'm a lone wolf. No pack. No friends. No mate. Nothing to protect. Nothing to love. Nothing to make me weak."

The pack makes us strong, not weak, whispered his wolf from inside as Caleb felt himself beginning to Change back into a man. *And a mate makes us all-powerful. It balances the darkness in us, puts us in control of our destiny, in line with our fate.*

Caleb howled once more as he tried to get his wolf to shut up, and then suddenly he was a man again, whipping his body upright and straightening out so fast he almost fell flat on his face. But he kept his balance, his bare feet barely touching the burning sand as he sprinted deeper into the desert, the sweat pouring down his glistening naked body, his chest heaving with the strain of going full-tilt over the sand dunes. For a moment he thought he could just run himself to death, end the conflict and confusion that was driving him close to madness. But although there had been dark days when Caleb had considered ending it all, he couldn't access those feelings anymore. Dormant instincts were waking up, and he couldn't fight them any longer. He had needs to protect, to mate, to love. He needed his pack, his crew, his brothers. He needed his mate.

His mate.

And as he finally let the nagging thought erupt to fruition in his mind, he saw an image of Magda. Except it wasn't that rail-thin, dark-eyed, pale-faced Magda he'd seen with his eyes. It was the woman inside her, the woman she really was, the woman behind the veil, behind the facade, behind the curtain. She had the same eyes, but they were full of life and warmth. The same face, but filled out and glowing with a warm smile. The pale, sunken cheeks were now round and rosy. Her body pushed against her shapeless robe, breasts and hips rounding out the cloth and making Caleb pant as his eyes went wide, his body tightened, his cock stood straight out as he ran naked through the desert.

He felt himself yearn for that woman, that image of Magda that he was certain was just a mirage of the desert, an hallucination thrown up by his frazzled mind. But still he reached out to her, and then he felt her magic wind its way through him as he raced through the desert.

A moment later everything went dark, and he could feel his body enveloped in that dark light until the sand was gone from beneath his feet, the blue sky disappeared, and Caleb was spinning in the air like a dust-devil as the witch drew him back to her.

4

"**P**ut some clothes on, please," she said coldly, trying not to stare at the naked soldier who'd spun himself into existence on the sandstone floor of her marble mansion. "There are children present."

Magda tried to keep her eyes dead and cold, but she could feel the heat rising along her body, a heat that made her uncomfortable, a heat that was unfamiliar, a heat that was undeniable.

She gasped as she felt a strange tightness in her chest, a tingling in her thighs, a trembling in her buttocks. Caleb was standing before her in all his glory, his eyes the midnight blue of the ocean, his body bronzed from the desert sun, the tattoos that covered his contoured muscles all spelling out her name, it seemed. She blinked as she tried not to stare between his legs, at his swollen manhood. But it was hard to ignore. He was ramrod straight, thick and heavy, and Magda's eyelids fluttered as she tried to keep her eyes on his face even as her mind whipped up images of him putting that thing inside her, holding her down and pumping her from behind, those heavy balls of his emptying inside her cold depths, heating her up to the point of explosion.

"Clothes!" she said again, turning away from him and swallowing hard as that strange tightening in her breasts, ass, and thighs made her robe begin to press against her body, press against her . . . curves?

No, she thought in a panic as she looked down at herself, half-expecting to see her boobs popping out, her ass expanding, her thighs thickening. But although it felt like that, she was still that rail-thin woman. It was her imagination. She wasn't going to suddenly turn into that self-conscious, oversized girl who'd been teased and taunted to the point of despair. She was powerful now. Living the dream of every girl who'd struggled to fit into her pants, struggled to fit into society, who'd been teased or bullied or worse.

"The children don't seem to give a shit," came Caleb's voice, smooth and deep, cutting through her paranoia and adding a different sort of nervousness to her inner turmoil. "I doubt they've ever seen their father and mother *with* clothes! They have the un-prejudiced acceptance of nakedness like every animal does, Magda. Every animal except you, it appears."

"Because I'm not an animal," said Magda firmly—almost too firmly. Again her heart leapt at a long-buried memory from childhood. A memory of her running through the forest, every sense heightened, a feeling of divine freedom flowing through her. A feeling that had been stolen from her. Taken away. Murdered.

"Humans are animals too," said Caleb, making no move to cover himself. "You *are* human, aren't you?"

Magda snorted softly, turning back to him and looking into his eyes. Damn, they were so blue. So deep. So perfect. "You don't want to know what I am. Now put some clothes on or I'll dress you myself."

Caleb's blue eyes widened, and he put his hands on his hips and grinned. "Really? *You'll* dress me? With magic? Now that sounds like a neat trick!" He looked down at his erection and frowned. "Nothing too tight, though. This guy needs space to—*ouch*! What the hell?!"

With a wave of her hand and the whisper of a simple spell, Magda conjured up a set of shining metal underwear, reminiscent of a thirteenth-century chastity belt, complete with an oversized iron padlock dangling dead center. She giggled as she watched Caleb stare down at himself in shock, then look back up at her, his face going bright red with a mixture of anger, surprise, and perhaps just a bit of amusement.

"You really are a wicked witch," he grunted, flipping the padlock up and staring down at it. "Where the hell did you even come up with something like this?"

"Royals in the old days had their daughters wear these," Magda said, her eyes twinkling as she watched the lean, muscled Navy Seal scratch his buzzed head as he stared down at the chastity belt and its enormous padlock. "Just so no frisky knight got any ideas."

Caleb grunted. "Well, I wasn't getting any ideas," he said, looking her up and down and shrugging. "You aren't my type."

Magda blinked, feeling that tightness in her chest and ass again as if her body wanted to pop out into its natural form, as if something inside her was saying, "Yes! I *am* your type!"

You are his type and he knows it. He sees the woman inside the robe, behind the veil, past the facade, came a voice from inside her, and Magda almost choked as she heard it clear as day. It was the same voice she'd heard as a child, a voice that was hers and also not hers, a voice that belonged to something inside her, something that had come out into the open that night when she was still a child. The night before everything changed.

You're dead, she thought. They killed you. You're dead.

She held her breath, closing her eyes as she waited for a response. But none came. It was her imagination. Just traumatic memories playing havoc with her mind. Good. That she could handle.

You know what else you can handle, came the voice again just as she'd begun to calm down. *Pop that padlock off and show him that your cold, bony fingers are soft and warm, that this is just an illusion, that this is all a costume. Release him and let him smell our scent, our heat, our need. Then he will do the rest.*

Our scent, Magda thought as she felt her breaths come in gasps. Who is *us*? You're dead! They killed you in that government laboratory, with those drugs that were supposed to cure the Shifter disease. They killed you!

That's what they thought too, whispered the animal from inside her. *But here I am. And here he is. Your fated mate. He has brought me back from the dead so we can create new life. Back from the dead! Boo!*

"Boo!" came a high-pitched voice. It was one of Adam and Ash's twins, the little girl. She was grinning wide and clapping her chubby little hands as she stared at Magda and said, "Boo!" again.

Caleb turned to the twins, and Magda saw a dark cloud pass through him clear as day. Suddenly the unexpected, almost flirty atmosphere was gone, and Caleb turned back to her, his expression dead serious.

"What is it?" she said. "What did Murad say?"

"You know what he said," Caleb growled, his face tight and hard. "He wants me to kill them. He's scared of his own son—as he damned well should be. And we should be scared too. Why hasn't Adam found us yet, anyway?"

Magda turned to the balcony and sighed. She looked out over the rolling dunes of the desert, closing her eyes and muttering the spell she'd been using to obscure the location of the children. "I have been using a spell to keep the children hidden from the dragon's instincts to home in on its blood. But the spell will not last long. Sooner or later the dragon will pick up their trail and come for us." She turned to Caleb, blinking as she felt that dark power fill her like a vessel from the inside. This is about something bigger than you, she reminded herself. Whatever you lost when they killed your animal was gained when you found the power of darkness, when you basked in the strength of magic.

I'm not dead, came that voice from inside her again, and Magda almost cried out in surprise as she felt her animal reaching out . . . reaching out for him. Reaching out for its mate. And even if I were, we both know that even death cannot stop fated mates from coming together. And it is coming together! All of it! We can have it all. We can both have it all. Our mate. Our children. The world itself.

Again the visions of that night when little Magda had first Changed came rushing back into her, and Magda swooned as she turned away from the balcony. Suddenly her head was spinning, and she felt herself falling . . . falling . . . falling . . .

"Got you," came Caleb's voice, and she gasped as his strong arms circled her waist and pulled her into his body. His scent was as strong as his grip: musky, masculine, wolflike. She breathed deep, feeling her animal thrash inside her like it was going wild. There was no denying it, she realized as her sight narrowed to a tight focus where she could see nothing but Caleb's eyes, blue eyes the color of midnight. No denying that her animal had come alive, that she was no longer just a dark witch but a dark Shifter witch.

"Yes," she whispered as the heat flowed through her, the energy of her animal mixing with the darkness of her magic, the currents swirling together like snakes. "Yes, you do have me, Caleb. Listen, I must tell you something. I need to tell you something." She paused, knowing that if she kept talking, there'd be no turning back. If she was wrong—wrong about herself, wrong about him, wrong about this—then the only solution would be . . .

"I already know," he said softly, his eyes flashing a blue so deep Magda almost spun back into that stupor. "I already know."

And then, with the desert sun blazing down on the witch and the wolf, two dragon-babies staring in innocent wonder, he kissed her.

By the eternal Shifter spirit that can never die, he kissed her.

5

At first he felt all the energy drawing out of him like his life itself was being drained, and Caleb almost choked as his eyes went wide. But he stayed with the kiss, stayed with his faith, stayed with his need.

And then it happened.

She changed.

She changed into the woman in Caleb's vision, and he gasped in shock as she felt her body expand as he held her close. Her boobs popped out and slammed into his hard chest, her ass filled his big strong hands from behind, her cheeks turned round and rosy, full of warmth and innocence. Even her eyes changed,

and Caleb just blinked as he drew back from the kiss
and took in the sight of this woman in his arms, her
full, red lips glistening from the kiss.

"Holy shit," he muttered, blinking again as he wondered if this was just another magic trick. But he knew
it wasn't. He knew that everything else had been magic, but this was real. So real it took his breath away.
So real it made his knees weak. So real it made him
want to take her, claim her, possess her. "Holy *shit*,
Magda!"

"Don't look at me!" she shrieked, turning her head
away as her light brown eyes went wide. She tried
to push herself away from him, but his grip was too
strong, his need too desperate. "I'm hideous!"

"You're beautiful," Caleb whispered, his voice thick
with arousal as he looked down along her smooth
neckline, pausing at the divine sight of her cleavage
smushed against his bare chest. Her robe was straining at the seams, and with a grunt Caleb reached up
along her back and just ripped the cloth straight down
the middle, yanking it off her and tossing it across
the room just right so the thin robe landed over the
children like a blanket, hanging loose enough so it
was open from the bottom to let air in while obscuring the view of what was about to happen. Her feminine scent rose up to him like he'd just walked into
a field of flowers in bloom, and he took deep gulping breaths as he ran his bare hands down her naked
back, cupping her asscheeks with all his strength as

he pulled her closer against him. "Yes, you're beautiful, Magda. You're beautiful, and you're mine."

"I . . . I'm . . . you can't . . . don't . . ." she began to mumble, but Caleb stopped her with a vicious kiss, his lips smothering hers as he felt his wolf howl inside him, howl to the heavens, to the stars, to the moon and the sun and every planet in the universe. It had found its mate, and the human was taking care of business. It felt so right that Caleb would have howled out loud himself if he hadn't been kissing her so deep, so hard, so—

"Get this thing off me!" he roared as his cock strained against his metal cage. He reached down between her legs to feel her heat. God, she was wet, dripping, hot and ready for him. But he could feel the cold metal of that ridiculous chastity belt against the back of his hand as he fingered her between her legs, her scent almost making him dizzy as he felt his cock throb behind that padlock! "Get this damned thing off me, witch!"

Magda pulled away from the kiss, her eyelids fluttering as if she was going in and out of consciousness. Caleb shook her as he felt his wolf going crazy inside, threatening to come forth and break the damned padlock with its Shifter strength. Again Caleb shook her, holding her arms tight as she trembled like a curvy ragdoll in his grip, her eyelids still fluttering until finally they stayed open long enough for her to follow what he was saying.

She frowned and looked down at him, blinking and then giggling when she saw the metal underwear with the massive padlock holding back his manhood. Damn, she looked cute when she laughed! She looked up into his eyes and took a breath. Then she nodded and muttered a few words that Caleb couldn't understand.

And nothing happened.

Nothing.

Not a damned thing.

"Are you fucking *kidding* me!" Caleb roared, his head whipping back, his neck straining as he reached down and pulled at the padlock in anger. "You put this on me. Now get it off!"

"I . . . I can't!" Magda screamed, her eyes going wide as she muttered the spell again without any effect. "My magic isn't working! I . . . I don't know . . ." She frowned as she looked down at herself, cocking her head as something just occurred to her. Then she exhaled and closed her eyes, shaking her head and whispering something under her breath. "This is wrong," she whispered. "I can't do it. I have to resist. I can't lose my powers, lose my magic. I can't, Caleb. I'm sorry."

Caleb frowned as he felt a chill pass through him—a real chill, cold like ice. He realized it was coming from Magda, and he was startled when she opened her eyes again to reveal the black, dead eyes of the dark witch.

"No!" shouted Caleb, shaking her again as he watched her face morph back into the sunken paleness of the witch. "Magda! No! Come back! Come back to me!"

But it was no use, and Caleb howled in anguish as he felt her body shrivel up again, her beautiful curves receding like the tide, her lips going thin, her ass shrinking, chest flattening out, body getting lighter until she felt like a feather in his arms.

She pulled away from him, covering her skinny body as she ran across the room, grabbed her robe from the children's heads, and covered herself before turning back to him.

"What the hell just happened?" Caleb growled, his jaw tightening as he fought back his wolf, who was going insane inside him, its need to take its mate driving it close to feral madness. "I thought we were—"

"We can't," said Magda, shaking her head firmly, her cheekbones sharp like daggers as the sun lit her up and made her look so pale he swore he could see the dark blue veins streaking across her neck and forehead. "Not now. Not ever. There's too much at stake. If I lose my magic, then . . ."

"Why would you lose your magic?" said Caleb, rubbing his buzzed head as he paced the room like a wolf in a cage, trying to work off the energy that had built up from the arousal. He wanted to smash something. Bite something. Destroy something. He wanted to run, to howl, to feed, to . . . to *mate*! She was his mate! Couldn't she see that?! How could anything be more important than following that need?!

"I don't know for sure," Magda said, folding her arms over her chest, her jaw going tight. She didn't say anything else, and her brow furrowed as if she'd just thought of something. "But if my magic didn't work on you while we were . . . while you were . . . while *that* was happening . . ."

Caleb felt the chill of realization creep up along his back as he finished Magda's sentence. "Then maybe your other spells were broken too. Like the spell holding Murad's dragon in check," he muttered, blinking as he looked down at his hands and frowned. He thought back to how Murad's robe had glowed with the spell holding back his dragon, and then the chill turned into full-scale panic as he looked at the children. "Shit," he said. "We need to get the kids out of here, Magda. Because if your magic was turned off, then it's possible Murad's dragon broke through. And in dragon form he could track down his grandchildren, couldn't he? Track them down and . . ."

Magda opened her mouth to say something, but her voice was drowned out by a hideous screech that almost exploded Caleb's eardrums. A shadow passed across the room as if the sun had just gone behind a cloud, but there were no clouds in the desert sky.

"It's Murad!" Caleb shouted, glancing over at the

kids and then at Magda as every instinct in him came alive: The instinct to protect his mate, to protect the blood of his alpha, to protect his crew, his family. A moment later his wolf had burst forth, and he raced to the children and stood before them, teeth bared, claws out, every fiber on alert, every muscle in his lean wolf's body tensed and rippling as he prepared to fight to the death. He felt clear-headed in that moment, like there was no doubt about what he needed to do, about who he was, *what* he was. He was a soldier, part of a crew, and he would defend every member of his crew until he was torn apart and couldn't snap his jaws together again. He knew he didn't have a chance against Murad's dragon, but he didn't feel an ounce of fear. Perhaps he could hold off the dragon long enough for Magda's magic to get Murad under control again.

He glanced at the witch through his narrowed eyes, and he saw her step to the balcony and shout out the words to her spell. But the only response from the dragon was another screech that sounded like a thousand demons, and when Magda turned to him, Caleb knew her magic wasn't powerful enough to make Murad's dragon go back inside the man.

"Run," he growled to Magda, feeling that other instinct come alive: The instinct to protect his mate. "I'll handle this."

"He'll kill you," Magda said, shaking her head as she

turned back to the window. Outside Caleb could see the massive black dragon, its eyes like gold fireballs, its talons shining like pillars sharpened to deadly points. It had circled the mansion and was making a turn in the distance, preparing to smash through the walls and destroy everything inside. "He'll kill us all. It's over. I was wrong. I'm not strong enough. I was never strong enough. I'm still that awkward girl with the fat ass and big red zits. My magic isn't strong enough. I've failed. I was a fool. I—"

Caleb stared at the witch as his mind raced. Murad's black dragon had made its turn and was swooping in for the final attack. Already its maws were opening as it prepared to envelop the mansion with fire, and Caleb knew that although the speed of his wolf would allow him to get out in time, he'd never be able to do it with two kids and a woman on his back. Save yourself, or die with them. That's the only choice.

With a grin Caleb stepped away from the children, and a moment later he'd jumped at Magda, knocking her away from the balcony as he stood up on his hind legs to face the black dragon's onslaught. He wasn't fucking running! This was his mate, and the kids were part of his crew. His life wouldn't be worth shit if he turned his back on them. He was a soldier, a warrior, a protector, a defender. And what better way to go out than in a blaze of glory, teeth bared in defiance, claws shining and deadly in the last moment, eyes fearless and focused on the enemy! Bring it on, you big bird! Bring it *on*!

He saw the telltale wisps of blue flame swirl from the dragon's jaws, and he took a deep breath as he prepared to leap out from the balcony. Perhaps he could leap right into the dragon's mouth, run right down the overgrown bird's massive gullet, rip its throat and insides to shreds from within! Hell yeah, he could do that!

"See you in hell, witch," he growled to Magda, barely hearing her scream as he pushed off with his powerful hind legs and launched himself into the air.

"Not yet, Flying Squirrel," came a deep, rumbling voice suddenly, and Caleb roared in surprise as he felt himself knocked backwards in mid-flight. He landed on his feet, back on the balcony, and when he shook his head to clear it, he saw the second dragon.

It was Adam, and with his body the younger dragon blocked his father's flame, protecting his crewmate as he spread his gold and green wings like a shield. In a flash Caleb understood that when Magda had lost her magical powers for that short time, all her spells must have been broken—including the one obscuring the children's location from Daddy Dragon. He howled in delight at the sight of his old friend the dragon, going up on his hind legs and raising his paws as he considered leaping onto Adam's back to join in the fight!

"Protect my children," came Adam's deep voice through the dragon. "Take them and go. I'll handle Grandpa."

"We'll handle Grandpa together," growled Caleb, licking his chops as he felt the fever of a fight rushing through him. Damn, it felt good! Nothing like a good old ass-kicking to release all that pent-up energy from that mating fiasco.

And then images of Magda came rushing back to him, and he whipped his head around to where she was standing by the children. She seemed frozen, thin and pale, her lips moving but no sound coming out. Was she trying to cast another spell? Was she scared? Was there something else going on? Could she even be trusted?

"Protect my children," Adam said again, turning in the air and repelling another barrage of hot flame from Murad's dragon. Caleb could feel the heat almost singe his whiskers, and he knew this was no place for even a powerful wolf-shifter. Only a dragon could take on another dragon and hope to make it out alive. "And protect your mate."

Caleb turned back to Adam, his eyes wide, wolf-head cocked. Adam's head was turned, and Caleb swore he saw the massive dragon wink at him with those green-and-gold eyes of his old buddy, his military brother, his alpha. "How . . . how do you know?" Caleb growled, even though the battlefield was neither the time nor place for talking about women. Or maybe it was. He glanced back at Magda, then once more at Adam, who had just shot a fireball the size of the moon at his own father, who screeched as he whirled in the air to avoid the onslaught.

Once more Caleb felt the urge to join in the fight. He didn't give a rat's ass if he got burned to a crisp. He wanted in! But then he heard the children cry out as Murad's dragon swiped at Adam with a massive wing, sending Adam spinning in the air, spewing fire all over the place as he turned for a counter-attack.

"Get my kids out of here, you goddamn furball!" roared Adam. "That's an order, Soldier!"

The urgency in Adam's voice broke through to Caleb, and he finally nodded and ran back to where Magda and the children were standing—all the way inside the room, against the back wall. The mansion was made of black marble, and it wouldn't burn—not easily, at least. Caleb wasn't sure if there was *any-thing* that could withstand dragonfire for too long.

"We need to go," he barked at Magda. "Get the kids and climb on my back."

Magda didn't reply. She didn't move. She was just staring at the two dragons fighting in the distance, her pale lips trembling like she was a fish out of water. She looked like she was going into shock or something. Perhaps a trance. Or was she trying her magic again?

"Wait," he said as something occurred to him. "If

your magic is back, can't you just get us all out of
here to someplace safe? Spin us out of here with that
spell? What the hell are you waiting for? It's getting
hot in here, woman! Teleportation by magic is better than galloping through the goddamn desert on
my back! Do it!"

But Magda just stared at him, her eyes black and
cold, her lips frozen in a tight smile. Caleb couldn't tell
if she was out of her senses or if this was part of her
plan, if she wanted to watch the two dragons fight it
out until the world was reduced to ashes. Hell, maybe
she didn't want to get out of here! Maybe her magic
would protect her own skinny ass from dragonfire.
As for the kids . . . well, they were dragons, weren't
they? They wouldn't burn! They could be eaten, sure.
But Adam wasn't gonna let Grandpa chomp on his
kids for breakfast, so they weren't in as much danger
as it had appeared. Hell, the only one in real danger
was Caleb himself, he realized with a lopsided grin.

Once again Caleb felt like two paths were laid out
before him: Save your own furry ass and let the witch
do whatever she's got planned. Or stay here and . . .
and do what?! Die?

Caleb could feel his Shifter heart pound in his wolf-
chest, and as his big ears stood straight up, he thought
he heard the sound of another heartbeat. He frowned
and cocked his head, zeroing in on the sound until he
realized it was Magda's heartbeat. He'd never noticed

it before, and it puzzled him. Why the hell was he hearing it now?! *How* the hell was he hearing it now? After all, the air was full of screeching and crashing as the dragons fought each other in the open skies above the burning desert. The kids were screaming in fright. And the loudest sound in his wolf-head was the heartbeat of a cold, dark witch?!

She is our mate and there is no turning away from her, whispered his wolf through the chaos. *You have opened that door, and now you must step through it. There is no going back. She is ours, and we have to claim her. Nothing else will bring us peace. Nothing else will stop what is unfolding.*

And as Caleb listened to his wolf, he realized that his own heartbeat was in lockstep with Magda's, two hearts beating in time, two hearts beating as one. Again he looked into her dark eyes, wondering if he could trust his wolf, trust his heart, trust *her* heart! She was a dark witch, after all! She'd made a deal with dark powers at some point in her life, and Caleb knew enough to know that dark powers were . . . .well, *powerful*! She'd been strong enough to hold Murad's dragon in check, strong enough to imprison Bart the Bear, strong enough to bring Caleb himself to his knees. Wasn't Caleb better off getting the hell out of here so he could fight another day?

The thoughts came rushing in with the cool calculation of his military training. Common sense dictated that he was of no use to anyone if he was dead. But the sound of his heart and her heart beating in time was deafening, and when Caleb remembered what Adam had told him—*Protect my kids. Protect your mate*—he knew that common sense could go fuck itself. He wasn't going anywhere. Adam was his Alpha, and Magda was his mate. He wasn't going anywhere without them.

"All right," he muttered, shaking his furry head as tried to step towards her. But he couldn't, and with a grunt of surprise he realized he was frozen in place by her magic. He roared in frustration, and when he looked into Magda's eyes he realized that mate or not, she was all dark right now. She wasn't grabbing those kids and climbing on his back, and she sure as hell wasn't going to spin up a teleportation spell to get them the hell out of here. Which meant there was only one thing to do.

"All right," he said again, steeling his resolve as he prepared to do what seemed ridiculous. "If you won't use your magic, then we'll have to use my magic. Pucker up, witch. Here comes your wolf. Or rather, here comes your man."

He couldn't move, but he could still Change, and in a flash he Changed back to the man, standing up straight and tall, his muscled body ripped and tense, his jaw tight with resolve. He could feel the heat from the dragonfire searing his back, feel her spell binding his body from the front. But he gritted his teeth and fought with everything he had, somehow taking three steps towards his mate and cupping her face in his rough hands.

And as the dragons screeched and the babies screamed, as the dark witch stared up at him, her cold heart beating in time with his, he kissed her. He kissed her hard, with authority, the wolf claiming his witch with his lips, breaking her spell with his kiss. He kissed her. God-*damn*, he kissed her!

6

Magda could feel the dark power building up in her again, and she welcomed it just like she'd welcomed it all those years ago when her animal had been stolen from her, leaving a void that needed to be filled. Her lips were frozen in a tight smile as she watched the two dragons spin and twist in the air, shooting flames at one another, Adam's dragon spreading its wings to stop his father's dragonfire from reaching into the mansion.

This was the plan, she told herself as she heard the children scream from behind her. To release Murad's dragon, put it front and center with its own kind, its own blood, its son and grandchildren. It was the only chance Murad had to gain control over his beast; and he needed to gain control over his dragon if he wanted to command an army of Shifters. The children weren't in real danger, she'd told herself. Murad the man might have ordered Caleb to kill the children, but the dragon wouldn't allow its own blood to be executed! The dragon operated on instinct, no matter how twisted and dark it had become after years of being bottled up by magic. And the instinct to protect your bloodline was too deeply rooted to be overcome by cold logic. The instinct to protect your offspring was the foundation of all life, big and small, mundane and magical.

Along with the instinct to actually *create* your offspring, came the thought as Magda's attention wavered at the sight of Caleb standing guard at the balcony, his massive wolf's body looking magnificent and strong, giving her a sense of security that made her feel warm inside. She'd screamed when Caleb had leapt off the balcony, fearlessly heading for Murad's dragon and certain death. But then Adam had swooped in, and Caleb had headed back to her . . . headed back to her, Changed back to the man, and kissed her.

Kissed her!

Suddenly everything spun forward, and Magda blinked in confusion as she felt the heat of his lips against hers, heard his powerful heart beating in time with hers, felt her dark power once again recede to the background as if it couldn't sustain itself in his presence. She struggled as the conflict blazed through her along with the heat of arousal, the need of her animal, the need of her feminine.

If we give ourselves to him, do we lose our magic, came the thought from somewhere deep inside. She thought it was from that dark place, that place where her magic lived, that place in her soul which belonged to the dark powers with whom she'd made her deal all those years ago, when she was broken and angry, filled with hate and rage. They'd killed her animal, and she wanted to kill them back! Kill them all!

But your animal is still alive, she thought as she felt it inside her even as Caleb's tongue twisted into her mouth. Had it ever died? Was it all a trick? Was she tricked into making that dark deal? Tricked by whom?!

Tricked by me, came the whisper of her animal, and Magda gasped as her eyes flicked wide open with the shock of realization. *I'm a fox, honey. There's a reason for the saying "Sly as a fox." They wanted me dead, so I played dead. I played dead, and you found new life. With dark magic we're more powerful than ever. Fox-shifters don't have the brute strength of the bear or the blinding speed of the wolf. We're smart and sly, and that's our game, honey.*

"It was you," Magda whispered in confusion, her voice muffled as Caleb held her face tight and kissed her again. "*You* made the deal with darkness!"

Sly like a fox, whispered her animal. *You were too good and innocent to do it. You would have let those government scientists kill me with their drugs. Perhaps you would have let them kill you too. I made a deal with the darkness for your sake. For our sake. And look what it has gotten us, honey!*

What has it gotten us, Magda thought in despair as she felt her body pushing against her robe once more as Caleb kissed her harder even as the dragons fought in the background.

It has gotten us everything, replied her fox. *Power, good looks, and our mate!*

Except we lose our magic if we accept our mate, Magda thought. And without our magic, we're nothing. It all goes away. Even if Murad gains control over his dragon, without magic I'm of no use to him. He'll take control of his army and take over the world! His dragon's hoarding instincts will push him onward: He will claim everything as his, and destroy everything that stands in his way! That isn't the vision! The vision is to cleanse the world of evil, destroy the ones who hold prejudice and hatred in their hearts, return us all to the Garden of Eden. I need my magic to do that!

And you will have it, whispered the sly fox from inside her. *You just need to accept the darkness like I did. You're only losing your magic because the human in you never accepted the dark deal. It was me. I sacrificed for you, for us, for this. Now it's time for you to do the same, honey. Say yes and you'll keep your magic, keep your mate, and maybe even keep your tight little waistline! You'll have it all, honey! Just say yes. Say yes, little Magda. Say yes!*

"Yes," Magda mumbled as the heat from Caleb's kiss mixed with the heat from the dragonfire, all of it swirling together in a way that seemed to make perfect sense amidst the chaos. Man and woman had left the Garden of Eden because they'd taken a path of darkness, hadn't they? So perhaps the way back to the Garden was to walk the same path! Follow the same road and it'll lead you to the same place! Perfect sense! "Yes," she said again, this time with more confidence, her voice strong and steady. She could feel the dark power rise up again in her, but this time it felt different, more complete. In that moment she knew her animal was right: The human in Magda had never given herself completely to the darkness, which was why Caleb's kiss made her lose her powers. Shifters could only mate in human form, and her mate's kiss brought forth the woman in Magda— the human woman untouched by darkness but also stripped of her magic.

Maybe I *can* have it all, Magda thought as she felt her robe loosen around her, her body tightening into that rail-thin frame of the witch. My magic, my mate, and my vision of the world.

But even as she thought it, she felt her vision changing form as the darkness snaked its way through her
as Caleb kissed her deeper. Suddenly those old feelings of hatred for the people who'd tried to kill her animal returned front and center, and before she knew
it the only thing she could feel was hatred and anger,
the need for vengeance, the craving to destroy everything and everyone, all humans, good or evil. She
felt a cold clarity as she ran her fingers across Caleb's
buzzed hair, opened her mouth wider, laughing silent-
ly as she felt his tongue twist inside her like a snake.

Yes, she thought. Humans left the Garden of Eden
when they lost touch with their animal selves, when
they learned to be ashamed of their bodies. *Humans* are the problem—*all* humans! They *all* need
to go!

"We need to go," came Caleb's voice through her
insane thoughts, and Magda blinked when she felt
him draw back from the kiss. She didn't want him to
stop. She wanted him to take her now. Who gave a
damn if they were in danger of being burned alive by
two dragons fighting each other in the skies outside
their window! "Magda! We need to go now! Adam's
doing all he can to control his father, but the black
dragon is too strong. I don't know if—"

The rest of Caleb's words were lost as the thick
marble wall at the far end of the room crumbled like
a cookie as the massive wing of Murad's black dragon

came crashing through. Magda screamed as she saw the talons rush towards her and her mate, and she felt real fear then, real horror, real failure. All those years of using her magic to hold Murad's dragon inside had done more damage than good. It was like winding up a spring, and all that pent-up aggression was out of control. Suddenly she realized that the dragon might indeed kill its own grandchildren! It might indeed kill its own son! It was all dark, all destruction, all evil.

And it was all her fault.

She felt a ripple of conflict flow through her insides. It was almost like the darkness in her was fighting for full control, like there was still a part of her that hadn't given itself away. It made her feel sick, and her head spun as she tried to chant the spell that would take Caleb and her and the children to safety. But her words came out slurred, the spell powerless as the conflict raged inside her. She couldn't tell if it was because Caleb was near. She couldn't tell if it was because the human in her hadn't accepted the darkness all the way. She couldn't tell if it was her animal's conflict now that it was so close to its mate. All she knew was that she felt powerless, broken, confused. She needed her man. She needed her mate.

Magda opened her mouth to speak, to tell him she'd failed, that she'd started all of this and now she'd lost control. She wanted to say she was sorry, sorry that they were all going to die, die before they even got a chance to really live.

But she didn't need to say anything, because she could see the determination in Caleb's eyes, which were flashing that deep blue of the open seas. She felt a smile come across her face as everything slowed down for her, a strange peace washing through her body as those deadly talons of the black dragon swept their way across the room.

And then Caleb was a wolf again, the Change coming so quickly Magda gasped in shock. He crouched down and barreled into her legs, knocking her off her feet and forcing her to land on his broad, furry back.

"Grab the children and hang on," he growled through sharp fangs as white as snow. "Hang on for your goddamn life, woman, you understand?"

Without thinking Magda grabbed the twins and pulled them against her breast. They instinctively grabbed onto her with their tiny but strong hands, and Magda leaned forward on the wolf's back, driving her heels into him until she felt secure. The children were pressed tight between her and the wolf, and Magda clutched Caleb's thick fur as she felt the wolf break into a blindingly fast run.

Caleb leapt over the sweeping talons of the black dragon, heading straight for the gaping hole at the far end of the room. Magda stared as the wolf made no move to slow down, instead running straight through the hole and launching himself like a bullet into the air, high above the hard sand of the desert.

"What are you doing?!" Magda screamed into Caleb's ear as she felt the air rush against her face. "We're all going to die! We're—"

"It's called teamwork, babe," Caleb snarled as Adam's dragon came roaring in below them, controlling its flight perfectly so that the wolf landed squarely on its back, its claws digging deep into the dragon's scales. "Right, brother?" he yelled at Adam, his snout hanging open in a grin of pure delight. "Now get us the hell out of here, you overgrown parrot. Your dad still has some fight left in his hollow old bones. We might need reinforcements to win this one."

7

Caleb let his tongue hang out and flop against his snout as the dragon glided in for a landing atop the massive open roof of its lair in the Caspian Sea. The smell of the sea was like a drug to Caleb—he was a Navy Seal after all. What the hell had he been doing in the desert all these years, anyway?!

He turned his head halfway and sniffed the air, taking in the scent of the woman crouching tight on his back. He could smell her clearly, smell her feminine musk, her hair, her skin, everything. But there was also another scent mixed in, and he cocked his head as it came through stronger in the clean air above the Caspian Sea.

"You're a Shifter," he said matter-of-factly, the scent of her animal unmistakable now. Perhaps it was the clean air. Perhaps it was because he was free from the clutches of her dark magic. "A canine. Not a wolf. Fox? Yes, fox."

"I don't know what I am," Magda mumbled after a long pause, during which Caleb had heard her heartbeat speed up. It had made his heart speed up too, reminding him again that she was his fated mate, that their hearts shared the same rhythm, that they were bound together by destiny, made for each other whether they liked it or not. "I thought I did, but I don't."

"Stop being so melodramatic," Caleb shouted above the screaming air as they swooped down on the dragon's back. "We're free. We're safe. And we're together. What more can you ask for?"

"We aren't free, and we're certainly not safe," Magda replied. "Yes, Adam's dragon flies fast enough that Murad couldn't keep up and we lost him. But now that Murad is in dragon form, it's only a matter of time before his dragon tracks its own blood and finds Adam's lair. And then what?"

"Then we fight, right, Adam?" Caleb said with a shrug. "Adam flies Bart and me up there. We drop down onto the black dragon's back, where his fire and talons can't reach us. Then we just rip through his scales and eat his goddamn heart! A real heartbreaker of an ending, yeah?"

Adam turned his massive head and opened his maws. Wisps of white smoke came chugging out as the dragon laughed, and Caleb's wolf barked and howled in delight. Damn, it felt good to be with Adam again, Caleb thought. His mate on his back, the smell of the sea all around! Shit, this was heaven! How did it all work out so quickly for him?!

Be careful, whispered the wolf from inside. *She is our mate, but she is not what she seems. Her fox is not to be underestimated. Foxes are sly. They are thinking animals. Conniving. Creative. Always cutting deals to make up for their lack of physical strength.*

If she's our mate then nothing else matters, Caleb thought as the dragon landed on the white stone floor of the open terrace. He felt so damned happy right now that he was certain nothing could go wrong, nothing would go wrong, not now, not *ever*! He felt fresh and alive, and all he wanted to do was greet his military brothers, hug them in the flesh, and then excuse himself while he did what needed to be done with his mate behind closed doors.

Or in the open perhaps, he thought with a hungry grunt as he blinked in the blinding sunlight reflecting off the pristine white tiles of the open terrace. He leapt off the dragon's back, landing softly on all fours and crouching down so Magda could get off his back with the children. She felt light as a feather, and Caleb furrowed his furry forehead as he thought back to when he'd kissed her that last time back at the mansion, amidst all the chaos. He'd felt her body react to his kiss, and he'd been waiting to feel her curves pop out the way they'd done the first time. But it hadn't happened all the way, and she'd been that rail-thin witch in her fake body ever since. Still, he decided as he heard footsteps and voices in the distance: She was his mate, and everything would work out. That was what fate meant. Yes, foxes were notoriously sly tricksters, but they were still animals. Her animal would forget all its schemes and plans once it was claimed by its mate. It was as simple as that. They would mate. She would get pregnant. And then they'd figure out the rest of the story together.

Not that the rest of the story would matter once they had babies, Caleb thought as he felt the urge to create new life burn strong in him. Yes, babies. That was the endgame, wasn't it? Babies, babies, and more babies! Let the games begin!

8

So many babies, Magda thought as she sat quietly at the dinner table and looked around at the group. Everyone was in human form, cleaned and dressed like this was an event. There was Adam at the head of the table, his wife Ash at the foot, their twins at either side of her on high chairs, grinning wide as they ate seared meat—which seemed to be the only thing dragons liked to eat. Magda and Caleb sat on the left side of the long, oval table, and across from them were Bart the Bear and Bis the Leopard with their three girls, all of whom were munching away on chicken legs in perfect unison.

Magda glanced furtively at Caleb, blinking as she

quickly turned back to her plate and looked down. He looked so happy, so fulfilled, so full of life and purpose. They'd been around each other for months now, but it still seemed strange to be sitting here beside him at a table full of mated couples. She still felt the undeniable truth that Caleb was her mate, that since her animal was alive, it would seek out its mate by pure instinct. But actually *mating* . . . now that was complicated. There was so much at stake, wasn't there? Losing her magic? Losing what made her powerful? This wasn't the time, was it? Not when Murad's dragon was unleashed on the world. Yes, she hadn't been able to stop it back at the mansion, but her magic might still be useful. If Murad Changed back to the man, her magic would likely work to keep his dragon locked up again. She had to hold on to it. Hold on to that darkness just a little while longer.

She thought back to that conversation she'd had with her fox, about how she'd said yes to the darkness. Her fox had said if the human in her accepted the darkness, she'd be able to keep her magic *and* get her mate! It seemed like a dream now. Had it really happened? There'd been so much going on: dragons fighting, children screaming, her mate kissing her. Could she risk letting Caleb claim her? What if she really did lose her magic, her powers, leaving her with nothing but a fat ass and an animal she wasn't sure she could trust! No. She couldn't. She'd trusted no one but herself for her entire life, and this wasn't the time to start trusting anyone or anything else. Not her animal, not her mate, not the universe.

She glanced over at Caleb once more. He was laughing and joking with his buddies, throwing chicken bones at Bart the Bear, making the children squeal with laughter as they imitated Uncle Caleb until Bart the Bear was growling and giggling as he protected his face from the onslaught. Everyone was smiling and laughing, but Magda was silent and still. It made her feel evil, like she was deceiving him, deceiving them all. They'd already accepted her into their group, but she didn't feel like she belonged with these happy, complete people.

She pressed her gown against her thighs. Her legs looked like toothpicks covered in cloth, and she sighed as she thought back to how she'd changed to that curvy girl she'd left behind years ago. She looked up once more, surveying the other two woman in the room and then sighing again. They were voluptuous, curvy women, with heavy breasts and wide hips, strong thighs and thick arms. And they seemed just fine with it, both Ash and Bis wearing form-fitting gowns that only highlighted their curves instead of hiding them!

I could never do that, Magda thought, hugging her bony shoulders and shivering as the cool night breeze drifted in through the large open windows of the castle. I'm not like them. I don't have the confidence to pull that off. I need my magic to look like I do.

A strange chill went through Magda as she allowed that thought to swirl through her mind. Was she so desperate to hold on to her magic for the most superficial of reasons?! With all the power her magic had given her, was the power to make herself look thin the one she truly cherished?! Was she that petty, that shallow, that insecure? Had being teased and bullied as an awkward, oversized girl affected her so much that being thin was an obsession, some kind of mental illness now?

"You aren't eating," came Bis's accented voice from across the table. "Is there something wrong with the food? Can we get you something else?"

"We've got dessert coming up soon," said Ash from the foot of the table. Her round face was glowing as she said the word dessert. "You have a sweet tooth, don't you? Well, my frosted bear-claws will take care of that. Here, let me bring them out now."

"No, I'm fine," Magda said hurriedly, forcing a smile and then quickly picking up a chicken wing from her plate. "This is fine. I ate earlier, actually."

"Really?" said Caleb, frowning and cocking his head at her. "When? I've been with you for at least twenty-four hours straight, and I didn't see you eat a thing. Unless you used your magic to knock me out so you wouldn't have to share. Bad girl. Bad witch."

Everyone laughed, but Magda turned bright red,

the anger and shame rising in her as memories of being teased came roaring back through her like it was just yesterday. She thought back to those traumatic moments in the school lunchroom at the international school she'd attended in Europe. Kids from all over the world seemed to have one thing in common: The ability to bond together and pick on someone.

Massive Maggie, the British kids had called her.

Maggie the Most-est, the American girls had named her.

Maggie the Manatee, the Eastern European teenagers had added.

Maggie didn't even know what a manatee was, and she suspected those spoiled brats didn't either. But when she looked it up, she cried for an hour alone in the library. She'd felt so alone, so powerless, so humiliated in that moment that she wondered if she was going to just burst, just explode right there, Massive Maggie splattered all over the stacks! She'd stayed in the library that night, crying until she was out of tears, the sadness slowly turning to hate, the despair transforming to determination.

And that's when it happened: She Changed.

Right there in the empty library, with the half-moon smiling at her through the large windows, Massive Maggie Changed. The animal burst forth from her awkward, unwieldy body, a sleek red fox with a bushy tail and sharp eyes! It raced around the empty library, yipping and yelping in delight as Maggie felt its energy rush through her in a way that was so exhilarating she'd started crying again—this time with joy.

She'd burst out into the dark forest surrounding the school, bounding through bushes, jumping over rocks, swimming through little streams that looked silver in the moonlight. She felt so light and free that it was all she could do to stop herself from howling and yipping so loud that it would have woken up every girl and teacher in the school.

She'd raced through the woods all night, and when morning came she'd finally Changed back to the girl, her sleek fox disappearing. But that feeling of lightness had stayed with her, and the next day she just smiled as the other girls teased her. She smiled because it didn't seem to matter anymore. She had a secret, and they didn't matter. The humiliation and hatred was gone, and Maggie spent each day just waiting for nightfall so she could become that lightfooted fox again, become her true self, an animal that was pure instinct, with no place in its heart for hatred. Hatred was a human emotion, and Maggie wanted to be all animal.

For months she Changed back and forth unnoticed, spending her nights roaming the forests, in her element, exploring her animal self.

And then they found her.

And they took her.

They killed her animal.
Leaving nothing behind but the girl.
The girl and the hatred.

9

Caleb saw the hatred flash in her eyes as he made the quip about not wanting to share her food, and immediately he knew he'd messed up. Fated mates or not, the truth was they still didn't know each other as people. Sure, his wolf wanted her, but they were humans too, and the human mating ritual was slightly more complicated than the simple instincts of the animal to see its mate and then take its mate.

"Hey, I was just kidding," he said softly, reaching out and touching her thigh beneath the table. She recoiled at the touch, and Caleb frowned as he sniffed the air for the scent of her animal. He couldn't pick it up, which was strange. He was certain she was a Shifter—

he'd picked up the scent earlier, when they'd kissed the first time and then later when she was holding onto his back as they fled the scene at the mansion. But now it seemed like her animal was buried deep inside her—so deep that even his wolf couldn't find it. A chill passed through him when he remembered that this woman sitting beside him was also a witch—a dark witch. Yes, she clearly wasn't evil through-and-through, but there was still so much about her he didn't understand.

He looked around the room, frowning as he took in the sight of his crew and their mates—their wives and children. Had he put them in danger bringing her here? Was he still under a dark witch's spell? Was this part of her plan, to get Caleb to trust her, to bring her right into the dragon's lair, to put her in a position to . . . to . . .

Stop it, Caleb told himself, crunching absentmindedly on a chicken bone as his wolf stirred inside him at the thought of danger to his crew and their families. She is your mate, and there isn't any magic that can fake that connection.

"So when did you two realize you were fated mates?" came Ash's voice from the foot of the table. Clearly she'd seen that Magda was uncomfortable talking about food and eating, and she was changing the topic.

"They always knew," said Bis from across the table.

She smiled sweetly at both of them. "It didn't take me long to figure it out. How else would she have gotten this lone wolf to fall under her spell? No dark magic is powerful enough to control a Shifter like that. Not unless there's another kind of magic in play."

"You'd be surprised at what you can do with dark magic," Magda whispered, her voice low and smooth, cold darkness flashing in her eyes as she glared at Bis in a way that made Bis's face go white.

Caleb's wolf immediately went on high alert as it sensed every other Shifter in the room bristle as the tension ripped around the table. Ash's face had gone tight, and she'd glanced at her children and then looked up at Adam, whose eyes were glowing bright with the fire of his dragon. Bart the Bear had gone rigid, as if he was trying to hold back his Change, and Bis herself seemed coiled like the black leopard inside her was ready to defend her own.

"OK, time out," Caleb said, flashing a wolfish grin as he tried to break the tension. "How about that dessert, yeah? Get some sugar into the system?"

"No, thank you," said Magda, crossing her arms over her flat chest. "Not for me."

"You do the low-carb thing?" Ash asked, her gaze taking in Magda's wire-thin frame before she blinked and forced a smile. "I gotta try that sometime. What do you think, honey?" she said, looking at Adam, whose eyes were still glowing.

Adam had been staring at Magda with an intensity

that worried Caleb. He knew that Adam felt responsible for the safety of everyone in the room, and Caleb could feel the conflict in his Alpha. Yes, Adam did believe that Caleb and Magda were fated mates, but he couldn't just forget that she was also a dark witch. Adam had always been skeptical about the power of fated mates to overcome anything and everything, and perhaps some of that skepticism still remained. After all, he and Adam hadn't been in close contact for years.

Finally Adam let out a slow breath, wisps of white smoke curling in the cool air as he blinked and glanced over at his wife. "Low-carb? Well, I'm all about a high-protein diet, so I'm cool with whatever you decide. But you lose even an inch of those curves and there'll be big trouble."

Ash giggled as the tension seemed to drain from the room, and soon everyone was smiling. Everyone except Magda.

"This was a mistake," she suddenly said, standing up so quickly her bony thighs banged against the heavy wooden table. "I don't belong here. I'm not ready for this. I'm not a part of this."

"What the hell are you talking about?" Caleb said, pushing his plate away and standing to face her. "You're a Shifter, Magda. And you're my mate! This is your place! This is your family! It's going to take some time to get used to it, but trust me, it's going to work out just fine."

"You keep saying that, but it's not true!" Magda screamed, her eyes flashing pure black as Caleb stared. "Nothing just 'works out' on its own!"

"This does," Caleb said firmly, his eyes narrowing as his wolf rumbled beneath the surface, reminding him that he needed to claim her, take her, show her the power of fated mates—show them *all* the power of fate. "Come here, Magda. Show them who you are. Show them the true woman inside, the woman who showed herself to me when I kissed you that first time. Come here, I said."

He reached out to touch her face, to draw her into him, to kiss her and end this conflict once and for all. He needed to show everyone that Magda's dark magic would evaporate when confronted with the purest form of magic in the universe: The magic of primal instinct, the magic of physical touch, the magic of fated love.

But she pulled away from him, and as Caleb growled and reached out to grab her by the back of the neck, she muttered something and he went flying across the room with a force that knocked the wind out of him.

Instantly the room erupted as Bart roared in anger and stood up, his bear bursting forth. Ash had Changed too, and so had Bis, both the golden bear and the black leopard of the women standing protectively in front of their respective children. Only Adam remained in human form, as if he knew that he couldn't unleash his dragon in a confined space without destroying the building and everyone in it.

Caleb looked down at himself, expecting to see the familiar shape of his wolf. He'd felt his Change coming, but as he stared at himself he realized he was still in human form. He cocked his head and tried to move, but he couldn't.

"What are you doing?" he rasped through gritted teeth as he stared at Magda's dead black eyes, saw her pale lips moving as she uttered silent words under her breath. "Are you crazy? These are friends! Family! I'm your mate, Magda! Your man! You have to trust me! I'm your . . . your *fate*!"

"I trusted in fate once," she whispered, "and it brought me nothing but darkness and death. That's my true fate, Caleb. Darkness and death. Everything connected to me dies or turns dark. Sometimes both. You want to be a part of that? You want in?"

Caleb frowned, twisting his neck as he fought her magic, as his wolf strained to get out. It was growling and thrashing inside him, and he could smell the scent of Magda's animal respond. It was alive in her, he knew. He wasn't sure what she'd meant with all that talk of darkness and death. Yeah, she was a dark witch. But there was good in her. He'd seen it in those big brown eyes when he'd kissed her and broken through that veil, that facade, that damned witch's masquerade of sunken cheekbones and tooth-

pick-thin legs! He'd done it once, and he could do it
again. Again and again. Forever and ever. His wolf
knew she was the one, and he knew it too. Everything else could go take a flying fuck, for all he cared.

"Do I want in?" he snarled as he felt his wolf slowly
push back against her magic. "Darkness? Death? You
think that scares me, Magda? You think it scares anyone in this room? We've all seen darkness and death.
We've all *been* darkness and death at some point in
our lives! Hell, I'm surprised Adam isn't serving us
human meat for dinner! You know how many men
he's burned alive, swallowed whole, ripped to shreds?
And Bart—hah! Butterball here spent a decade running wild through South American villages! There
are legends being handed down about the fearsome
beast who crashes through the village gates in a feral
frenzy, killing, feeding, and . . ."

"And breaking things," Bart growled, licking his big
chops and shrugging with his massive bear shoulders.
"But I'm trying to get better."

Now Bismeeta spoke, her black leopard still in its
protective stance in front of its cubs, its long tail
moving side to side like a dancer. "The darkness can't
stand up to the light," she said softly, her voice sounding like a purr. "You saw how it turned out with Bart
and me. We gave ourselves to your dark magic, but
it couldn't get a hold on us. The magic of fated love
is more powerful than any deal with darkness. You

need to trust in it, Magda. Caleb's right. Trust him. Trust all of us. Trust yourself."

Magda blinked, her eyes flashing with that dark light as she glared at Bismeeta. "I can't trust myself," she hissed, and Caleb's wolf could sense her animal whispering inside her.

"You can trust your animal," Caleb said, his voice deepening as his wolf began to break through. "Your animal will never lie, will never mislead you, will never—"

Magda leaned her head back and laughed, the sound high-pitched in a way that made Caleb's wolf growl inside. He frowned as he sniffed the air again. She was a fox—he was sure of it now. Her animal was a fox, and it was whispering something to her from the inside! What was it saying? Was it telling her to trust him?

"My animal?" she snorted. "My animal is a trickster by nature. It lied to me for twenty years! All of you have animals that are physically powerful, and when you lose control over them it's obvious because you go crazy and break things or feed or whatever. But it's not so obvious when you can't control a trickster animal. Its game is to make you think you're in control . . . to the point where I don't know who I am anymore. I don't know *what* I am! Shifter or witch, good or evil . . . I just don't know!"

"I know what you are," growled Caleb, his neck

thickening, every strand of hair standing up as he felt his wolf poised to explode out of him. He could feel its strength, and he knew Magda's magic was weakening. She couldn't stop his Change. She was too turned around inside, too twisted by her internal conflict. And that meant she wasn't all dark, all evil, all bad. If she was, she'd have every dark power at her disposal. She was his mate, his fate, his goddamn woman. And he was going to show her that. End this drama now and forever. It was making his head hurt.

Do it, whispered his wolf from inside, and now Caleb knew why it was holding back. It knew Caleb the man needed to claim his mate in human form. Magda was right: She wasn't in control of her animal, and when you lose control of a sly animal like a fox, it takes control of your mind as much as it does your body. *Show the fox that it is an animal when it comes down to it, that it has needs that can only be met when it gives control back to the woman. Her animal is scared to give up control. The fox defends itself by subterfuge and trickery, by stealth and slyness. Make it howl, Caleb. Show it that you will protect it, protect her, protect the children you'll have together. Show her, Caleb.*

Caleb felt the energy surge through him, and his vision narrowed down to sharp points, tunnels of light at the end of which was nothing but his mate, his woman, his destiny. He couldn't give a damn who else was in the room. They could leave or they could stay—he didn't give a shit. Did a beast in the jungle give a rat's ass who else was around when it took its mate? The wolf pack reveled in the mating rituals of its members! There was no shame in it. He was a wolf, and his children would be wolves. Better get used to it, babe. Here I come. Man and beast rolled into one.

Every sense of Caleb's was heightened as he felt his heat rip through his hard, soldier's body. He had access to his wolf's sense of smell and hearing, its animal reflexes, its deepest instincts. He felt powerful in a way he never had, and in that moment he understood that it was because of her, because he was near her. Just being close to his fated mate brought his animal and human together in a way that felt exhilarating! He needed to show her how that felt, how it felt to have your animal and human in balance, the way it was meant to be!

But Caleb could see the conflict in Magda. She was turned around, twisting and thrashing inside. She didn't trust her animal, and perhaps she was right not to trust it. Caleb didn't know her full story. All he knew was that it was time for *their* story.

"Do you feel your animal's heat?" he whispered as he took another step towards her. "I feel it. I sense it. I damned well *smell* it!"

"It's a lie," she muttered, shaking her head violently as those green veins on her pale forehead throbbed. Her voice sounded different, as if it was the animal inside her speaking. Was her animal planting seeds of doubt in her mind?! Was that even possible? Wouldn't her animal know he was her fated mate?!

Caleb hesitated as the doubt crept in, and in that moment he saw a flash of red color whip across Magda's face like a swirl from a magical paintbrush. Suddenly her robe just collapsed in on itself, and out of the falling cloth burst a red fox, its eyes wide open like it was terrified, its bushy tail thrashing the air as it ran around the room like it was freaking out at being in the open!

The children laughed in delight as the fox raced around the room, jumping up on the table, knocking plates and glasses all over the place, forks and knives scattering all over the floor. It was clearly in a frenzy, out of its mind for being out in the open after what had perhaps been decades of hiding inside her.

And then, as Caleb stared in wonder at the beautiful animal inside his mate, the fox took a turn, gathered speed, and jumped straight out the open window facing the dark waters of the Caspian Sea.

Immediately Caleb's wolf burst out of him, and with a single leap he was flying after her, after his mate, his woman, his destiny. He had already launched himself into the air when he heard his buddy Bart the Bear calling after him, the words sounding muffled as the salty sea air whipped past his big wolf-ears:

"About time, Flying Squirrel," Bart was yelling after him, his bear-paws thumping on the floor in excitement. "Take her! Take her and claim her! Woohoo! Hell, yeah!"

"Yes," came Adam's voice, Caleb's wolf just about picking up the words as he narrowed his eyes and zoomed in on the red blur falling through the dark skies. "She's yours. And she's also ours. Part of our crew. Part of our family. So take her, and then bring her back. Bring her back, Caleb."

10

There's no going back, Magda thought as she twisted in the air, the wind screaming past her sharp fox-ears, her bushy tail helplessly swishing as she fell head-first towards the black water. No going back to the girl I used to be. I was wrong—wrong about everything. I don't know who I am, I don't know what I want, I don't know what I—

And then she yelped as a heavy body crashed into hers, the bulk of Caleb's gray wolf overwhelming her red fox, his strong paws clutching at her as the two animals spun in the air together.

"Let me go!" she screamed, her voice sounding strange coming from the snout of a fox. *Her* snout! "I want to die! I just want to—"

"I don't believe you," Caleb growled. He moved back from her snapping jaws and glared at her, his eyes the darkest of blues, shining like sapphires in the dim moonlight of the night. "Hey! Don't bite me, woman! I'm trying to save you!"

"It's pointless, Caleb. You can't trust me. How can you, when I can't trust myself, when I can't trust my animal, when I can't trust my magic! You've twisted me around, Caleb, and now I don't know which way is up!"

The wolf was wrapped tight around her small fox's body, and she could hear Caleb's heart pounding . . . pounding in time with hers. She could smell the salty air of the Caspian Sea, and she wondered how long they'd been falling, if they'd ever—

"This way is up," Caleb rasped urgently, grabbing her snout and pulling it upwards. "Now take a deep breath and hold it. We're gonna hit hard, and when we do, you need to Change back to a human. I don't want your fox scratching up my face when I'm swimming both of us back to the shore."

Magda blinked as Caleb's words rushed in along with a deep gulp of sea air, and before she had time for another thought the two animals crashed into the sea, fur and teeth and snouts and claws all rolled into one as the dark waves swallowed them up.

Magda felt the Change come the moment she hit the water, and although the impact almost knocked her senseless, Caleb's heavy body, tight muscles, and firm, protective grip took most of the force of the landing. She heard him grunt in pain as he used his powerful legs to break the surface of the water so the two of them could slide in without breaking every bone in their bodies, and it was only then that she realized how close they'd come to dying! Was she crazy?! Was her fox crazy?! Had her animal just launched itself headfirst from a castle window?! Weren't foxes supposed to be *smart*?!

Everything was black as Magda tried to scream, but thankfully Caleb's hand was over her nose and mouth or else she'd have swallowed half the sea. They were deep underwater, Caleb back in human form, naked and strong, holding her tight as he kicked with his legs and shimmied them back up the surface.

He held her face up above the water, his body tight and hard as he stayed upright and held her so her nose and mouth were above the dark waves.

"All right," he gasped, his lean, angled face lit up with excitement like he was actually having fun! Like diving into a dark sea from hundreds of feet up was actually something that this wolf-Shifter*enjoyed*! Maybe he was crazier than she was! "Now you can scream."

"What?" she gasped, feeling panic rush in as she tried to breathe but couldn't. "What's happening, Caleb?"

"You need to scream," he said calmly as Magda felt

a dizziness start to overtake her. "Scream your head off, woman. Do it!"

Magda felt herself losing consciousness, losing her grip, losing everything. She couldn't feel her magic, couldn't sense her animal, couldn't grab a hold of anything that had given her confidence, courage, and strength in the past. She felt weak, helpless, powerless, but just as the despair started to sink in, she opened her mouth and did what her man said.

She screamed.

She screamed loud, with abandon, opening her mouth wide and just letting it all go.

She screamed, the witch and the animal and the woman all joining together and releasing a bloodcurdling howl that she was sure could be heard through all seven dimensions of the universe.

Suddenly oxygen burned through her blood, and she felt her life-force spiral upwards so fast she screamed again, this time in sheer joy. Soon she was holding onto Caleb's hard body as he laughed and spun her around and around in the swirling waters, her head tilted back as she let every emotion fly up into the night air through her screeches. She didn't care how it sounded, didn't care that anyone listening might think she was either a crazy banshee or a screeching monster. She only cared about how it felt, and it felt good, so damned good.

"There we go," said Caleb, grinning as she finally stopped screaming and stared at him, her eyes open so wide she thought they might pop out of her head. "Feels good, doesn't it? Screaming is actually a life-saving mechanism in a life-or-death situation. It forces fresh air into your lungs. You were going into shock after the fall, and you would have passed out if you hadn't screamed like the crazy witch that you are."

"Did you just call me a crazy bitch?" she said, frowning as the waves crashed around them.

"No, I said witch," Caleb yelled into her ear. "*Witch*, not bitch!"

Magda laughed as she wrapped her arms around his strong neck and leaned her head back. She could feel her hair long and wet against her naked back, and she frowned as she tried to look down at herself in the dark water.

"Why am I naked?" she said.

Caleb laughed. "You haven't Changed in a while, have you?" he said. "Your fox doesn't need to wear clothes, so I think your gown is on the floor of the dining hall up there." He grinned and raised an eyebrow. "I'm naked too, if that makes you feel better."

"It does not," said Magda firmly, kicking her legs out and frowning again when she realized that her thighs and butt felt surprisingly strong beneath the waters. "Wait, why do I feel so . . . so buoyant? Am I . . . is my body . . . oh, God, I'm a *whale*!"

She felt the blood rush to her face as she looked

down at herself and realized that her boobs were smushed up against Caleb's tattooed, naked chest. Boobs. Big and heavy, with an ass and thighs to match!

"A whale Shifter? That's a new one," Caleb said innocently, reaching one hand beneath the surface and tenderly grabbing her ass. "Let me check. Hmmm. Interesting."

"Get your hands off me!" Magda said, laughing as she wriggled her ass beneath the waters. She could still feel the lingering embarrassment of being back in the body she thought she'd left behind years ago, but she also felt strangely secure as Caleb's strong hands cupped her big bottom like it was a perfect fit.

"As you wish, Witch," Caleb said, immediately pulling his hands away from beneath her and letting her sink a few inches into the sea before grabbing her again.

"OK, get your hands back on me!" she shrieked as the water rose above her chin and she kicked out desperately with her legs. "I can't swim!"

"All animals can swim," Caleb said with a laugh, grabbing on to her and holding her tight.

"Then why did you tell me to Change back to a human?" she demanded.

"Because I swim better as a man. Also, my wolf doesn't like to get its fur wet," Caleb said. "Takes a long time to dry out, and I left my hair-dryer upstairs."

Magda laughed as Caleb spun her around slowly in

the warm waters of the Caspian Sea. The moon was out now, a sharp, silver crescent that looked like a smile in the dark blue skies above. The black waves around them were shining, and although Magda had never been a water-person, she felt safe and protected with Caleb. Safer and more protected than she'd ever felt with her magic.

Perhaps there *is* something to this fated mates thing, she thought as she looked into her mate's blue eyes. Something that has to be experienced to be understood. Perhaps there is another kind of magic here, a magic more powerful than dark magic. After all, that's why my magic couldn't get a deep hold on Bart and Bis, right? Because their acceptance of each other unleashed a light that overcame the power of my darkness. Is that what's happening here? *Can* that happen here? Do I *want* it to happen here?

Magda felt her animal turn inside her as her thoughts swirled like the dark waves around them. She could feel the sly mind of her fox at work, but she could also sense that it was conflicted, that it was feeling the magic of being close to its fated mate, that its own schemes and plans were being upended by what it felt like to be held by Caleb, protected by Caleb, claimed by Caleb.

Loved by Caleb?

"Oh, right, you're a Navy Seal. You love the water," she said, forcing herself to speak before she lost herself in thought, before her mind got twisted up in the madness that was her life: Murad's dragon unleashed, Shifter armies running wild, crazy ambitions to take over the world, deals with dark powers that would have to be made good on. It all seemed like a dream, a fairy-tale, dark and twisted and unreal.

Perhaps it *was* unreal! Perhaps it was all over! Maybe the dark powers that her fox had made the deal with years ago had decided to leave her alone! Maybe those dark powers just wanted Murad's dragon to be unleashed, and now her own debt was paid! She'd found her mate, her animal was back, and maybe this was her happily ever after! Who cared whether Murad's dragon burned its way across the world! It wasn't her fault, right? If anything, the world owed *her* a debt for holding Murad's dragon in check all these years!

"Not really," Caleb said.

"What?" said Magda, blinking as she pushed away the thoughts that threatened to drown her more than any waves ever could. "Not really what?"

"You said I'm a Navy Seal so I must love the water. I actually became a Navy Seal because I was afraid of water as a child, because I decided at some point to face every fear of mine head on. Face it and defeat it," he said with a half-grin. "Got water in your ears, Witch?"

"Stop calling me a witch," she said, feeling self-conscious in a way that sent a strangely comforting chill through her body. It was like she was a teenager again, awkward and unsure, but somehow not ashamed—like she felt accepted this time around.

"Are you not a witch now?" Caleb said with a grin. "Magic powers gone? Dark powers dispersed by my magical touch?"

Magda giggled as she felt his fingers claw at her ass, slowly making their way to her rear parting. She gasped as a sudden wave of heat whipped through her, and even though she was already wet from the sea, she could feel her own wetness between her legs.

"Stop trying to change the subject," she said, blinking as she felt Caleb's hardness brush against her naked mound as he spun her slowly around like they were on a dancefloor beneath the open skies.

"This *is* the subject," Caleb whispered, pulling her closer, his breath warm on her wet face, his hardness pressing up against her mound and making her wetness flow faster. "You and me. It's time, Magda. Time for me to—*ouch*! What the hell?! Oh no, you didn't! You did *not* just do that! Oh hell, you're gonna pay for this!"

Magda giggled like the silly teenager she felt like, and Caleb just leaned his head back and shouted in amused frustration as that metal chastity-belt with the iron padlock popped back into existence, locking his cock and balls behind an inch of studded armor.

"This isn't funny," Caleb growled, leaning in close

to her neck, his breath hot against her skin.

"Really? Because I'm laughing," she whispered back through a wide smile. She reached between them and grabbed the padlock, raising it and letting it drop back against the metal underwear.

"Let me out, or I let you go," he said sternly.

"Is that a threat?"

"It's an order."

"Oh, an order?! Is taking orders from you part of the whole fated mates deal? I'll have to look up the rules to see what I'm signing up for."

"The only rules are the ones I make, Witch," Caleb growled, slowly running his tongue along her neck in a way that made her almost burn up with heat. She wasn't sure how the hell she'd managed to conjure up that medieval metal monstrosity without chanting a spell, and it was only when she felt her fox twist and turn with gleeful laughter that she understood that the little rascal inside her had done it! The horny little animal was . . . was *flirting*! Playing with its mate like a puppy or a kitten! Doing a dance of courtship! Testing its mate just like a woman tests her man! Putting up barriers just for the thrill of watching her man tear them down with his desire to claim his woman! And how the hell was her magic working when she was still in this shape with big boobs and a thick ass? Or was it not her magic but her fox's magic? Who knew. Who the hell knew. All she knew was that she was naked, being held by a man in metal underwear, and laughing her ass off like she was crazy!

"You like calling me Witch, don't you?" she said, smiling as she held on tight to the back of his thick, muscular neck. She ran her hand over his perfectly shaped, buzzcut head, his thick brown hair spraying her with saltwater as she rubbed it. "Wolf," she said softly. "You like calling me Witch, don't you, *Wolf . . .*"

"Yes," he whispered, drawing close, his thick stubble brushing up against her face and making her hot inside, so hot she thought she could boil the sea itself if this went on too long. "Like most horny schoolboys, I always fantasized about having sex with a witch," he said matter-of-factly.

"Must have been an interesting school," Magda said with a laugh. Then she reached beneath the water and knocked on his metal boxers. "Though nobody's having sex yet, I should remind you. I'm not that kind of witch. You'll need to buy me dinner first."

Caleb growled as he reached around to the back of her neck and grasped her firmly, holding her head back and looking down into her eyes. "Not that kind of witch, huh? Perhaps I'll just dunk you and see if you sink or float. That's how they did it in the old days, right?"

"Don't you *dare!*" she squealed, gasping as Caleb pulled her down just enough so the water lapped against her chin. "I'm afraid of water, Caleb. I swear I'll turn you into a goddamn frog!"

Caleb shrugged. "I'm a Navy Seal, Witch. They already call us frogmen. And if you can't swim, then turning me into a frog isn't gonna help your case, I should point out." He grinned and cocked his head. "Also, if you can't swim, why the hell did you jump into the sea? Got a death wish, Witch?"

Magda blinked as she felt her fox stir inside her. It was restless but quiet in a way that puzzled her. It had been so long since she'd felt its presence that she couldn't quite tell what was normal. Yes, she could feel its desire, its need to be claimed by its mate. But there was conflict too, conflict that the fox was hiding from its human. Was that even possible? Wasn't her fox just a part of her? Wouldn't she know everything her fox would know?

"The only thing I wish is that I'd never . . ." she started to say, the memories of that dark time in her life coming rushing back to her. Suddenly that playful, flirty atmosphere seemed lost, and now the waves felt ominous and dark, the moon's crescent like a grimace of pain, the wind that was once whistling now sounding like a whisper of warning. " . . . never made that deal."

"Deal? You mean with Murad?" Caleb said.

Magda sighed. How could she even begin to explain herself to him? How would he ever understand? How would he—

You don't need to explain yourself, whispered her fox suddenly, and when Magda heard its soft voice come through clear as daylight, she knew it had been listening to everything, sitting there on its haunches in her subconscious like the little fiend it was, taking it all in. *Not to him, at least. He is our mate, and he already understands, even if he does not know the details, even if he does not understand that he understands.*

Oh, so you're a philosopher now? Talking in riddles? Magda replied in her mind, almost rolling her eyes as she felt Caleb's strong arms hold her as he kicked out and slowly began to pull her back towards the island.

Above them the moon had gone behind a cloud, casting a gray-silver glow over the dark waves that lapped around them, and Magda shivered as she realized that they'd been in the sea for a long time now. She was glad Caleb was heading for shore. She was glad Caleb was with her. She was glad Caleb was . . . hers?

He's mine, she thought as her animal went silent again and Magda just held on to her mate as he swam them both towards the shore of the island. She could see the castle looming on the cliff face above them, and she wondered why the other Shifters hadn't come after them. She didn't see the dragon flying around, lighting the night sky with its flame. She didn't see anyone staring out of the windows or balconies. Did they even care? Were they glad the witch was gone? Perhaps. Perhaps they were just being polite letting her sit at the table with them. After all, they couldn't possibly trust her, could they? Couldn't possibly *like* her!

"You didn't answer my question," came Caleb's voice, soft but steady, without any indication of the effort he must have been exerting to swim against the current and pull them both back to safety. He was barely even breathing hard, she realized with awe as she felt his muscles flex and relax with each smooth stroke.

Magda felt herself relax as she concentrated on Caleb's body moving beneath the waves, his body moving against her body, protecting her, guiding her, leading her. Her head was buzzing as she lost herself in the rhythm of the two of them moving together, and soon she was aware that their breathing had fallen into lockstep, their hearts beating in time. She could feel the power of the physical, the flesh, the body. She could sense the simple beauty of two animals moving as one.

This is magic too, she thought as she tried to push away the nagging thoughts of that dark deal her fox had made to protect itself, to protect its human, to protect its . . . future?

Its future, Magda thought as Caleb got them closer to the shore, his powerful strokes guiding them around jagged rocks until she saw a patch of hard sand at the foot of the cliff—a tiny beach nestled into a cove. What future does an animal think about? Animals aren't burdened with far-reaching plans of some imagined future, are they? No. To an animal, the future means just one thing:

Reproduction.

Offspring.

Babies.

The moment the thought hit, Magda felt her fox tighten and twist inside her like it had been struck. She frowned in the darkness as she tried to get her animal to speak to her, to open up to her, to reveal what it was hiding from her, what it had been hiding from her for decades. She'd always known that her dark powers had been granted to her in exchange for something—that was how dark magic worked. You made a deal.

What was the deal, she asked her animal as Caleb's legs finally hit the seabed and he stood up, lifting her out of the water like she was a feather. She felt the water dripping down her long dark hair, rolling off her smooth curves, beading on her breasts like dark diamonds. She looked down at her naked body as Caleb carried her, gasping as she saw a vision of herself with a round belly, breasts heavy with milk, a new life forming inside her womb. Her child. His child. Their child. Their first-born pup.

"No," she muttered, feeling her fox yelp and thrash

inside her, her vision turning red as the animal whipped itself into a frenzy. That vision of hers became clearer as her mate carried her onto the dark sand of the hidden beach . . . clearer and darker . . . so clear and so dark that she almost choked. "What did you do? What did you promise?"

I had no choice, yelped her fox from amidst its frenzy, and now Magda understood that her animal was being turned inside out with conflict now that it had met its mate, now that its natural instincts to produce new life was so overwhelming that it couldn't be resisted. *Dark powers only make two kinds of deals. Either they want death, or they want new life. And I promised them both in return for the power of dark magic. We would give them death at the hands of your army. And we would also give them life. New life. Our first born.*

Magda almost howled out loud as her fox wailed inside her. She understood now that back then even her animal was young, innocent in a way, desperate to save itself and its human. The future seemed so far away, and it was so easy to say yes, sure, whatever you want in exchange for what we need now!

Except now the future is here, Magda thought as it occurred to her that the metal underwear that had started as a joke, a tease, playful flirtation was in fact her subconscious trying to delay the bill-collector. Yes, the future is here and you don't want to pay up.

Her fox yelped in anguish, and Magda sensed its innocent despair. She couldn't blame her animal, she realized. Her animal had done what it needed to do to save them both, and now it was her turn to step up. They were a team, Magda and her fox.

We're a team, my little red furball, she told her fox as she tried to get it to settle down. You, me, and our wolf. We'll find a way out. There's always a way out. There's always a way.

11

"**N**o way," Caleb said, standing with his hands on his hips and looking down at the big padlock blocking his cock. He shook his head and rubbed his jaw, feeling the saltwater roll down his neck as he tried to process what Magda had just told him, her words coming out like a tidal wave of information that threatened to drown his brain. "Deals with dark powers? Delivery of millions of dead human souls? Oh, and our first born child as a bonus payment? What is this, a goddamn *Harry Potter* knockoff?"

Magda cocked her head and frowned. "Was all of that in *Harry Potter*?"

"I don't freakin' know! Do I look like I read children's books?" Caleb roared, rubbing his head and pacing on the hard-packed sand of the little beach. "All right. All right. All *right!*" he said, taking long breaths as he steadied his heartrate like he'd been trained to do at Seal bootcamp. "Here's what we're gonna do. We're heading back to the castle, and we're going to set up a plan with the crew. We've got knowledge, resources, connections. We can figure this out together. All of us together."

Magda shook her head slowly, glancing up at the castle and then into Caleb's eyes. He could see that she was scared. Scared, guilty, and ashamed.

"I can't face them," she said softly. "I can't face your crew. Those other women. They'll see me for what I am."

"What you are is my mate," Caleb said firmly, his eyes narrowing as he looked down at Magda sitting on the sand, her legs drawn up close to her body. "And you're wet and cold. Stop being so dramatic and let's go back inside. Come on. Get up. You've got nothing to worry about. No one is going to take our first born child. Not while I'm still standing—and trust me, I'll *always* be standing between you and whatever demon, devil, ghost, or goblin wants to steal my babies." He tried to smile as he tapped his cocklock and winked. "Babies that still have to be made, I should remind you."

Magda smiled back, but Caleb could see the fear in her eyes. The metal underwear was no longer a joke, he realized. This woman was really and truly afraid that if she got pregnant, some mysterious dark power was going to show up and say, "The child is mine! Bwaahahahahahah!" What the hell, man. Benson didn't prepare me for this shit!

He reached for her hand, but she stayed in that curled up position, arms around her bare legs, sand between her toes, round face peering up at him. She looked like a scared child in that moment, not a dark witch with plans to conquer the world, and Caleb blinked as he wondered if this was all a trick, if the fox and the witch were making a fool out of the wolf and the soldier. After all, he'd been under her spell for two years. Was it broken just because they'd recognized that they were fated mates? Maybe. But maybe not. He didn't know much about dark magic.

You don't know that much about her either, Caleb reminded himself as he drew back his outstretched arm and looked up at the massive white castle, half-lit in the dim moonlight. You might be putting everyone up there in danger if you bring her back there. It would be fine if it were just Adam and Butterball the Bear. But they've got their mates up there too. Babies and cubs. It could become a volatile situation, he realized as he thought back to how the women had instantly Changed to their animals when their babies might be threatened, how Bart had let his bear out, how even Adam had to fight to stay in control of his dragon when Magda had used her magic briefly.

No, Caleb decided, his jaw going tight as he turned

back to Magda. The time will come when I'll need my crew, and they'll be there for me when that happens. But right now it's just me and her. Me and my mate. Just the two of us.

"All right, we won't go back up there," he said softly, frowning as he realized they were both naked, with no money, supplies, or means of transport. Could Magda conjure all that stuff up? Not right now, he decided. And I don't want her to access her dark magic right now anyway. This is on me. I'm gonna take care of this.

He took a breath and nodded slowly as he scanned the surroundings. He knew Adam well, and this little beach nestled into the foot of the cliff seemed a bit too artificial to be believable. After all, it was just rocks everywhere else on this side of the island, and as Caleb looked beneath his bare feet, he could tell that the sand itself looked dark, almost black.

"Sonofabitch," he muttered, looking closely at the sand and realizing that it was indeed artificial! It had been created from pulverized rock! Adam's dragon had built this beach by crushing the rock shoreline and then scorching the damned Earth until it turned into black sand! This wasn't a beach! It was an escape route! Which meant . . .

He squinted as he peered towards the far end of the beach, and then he saw it: The mouth of the cave. "Hell yeah, Adam," he said with a grin. "Always prepared. Always a plan."

"What is it?" Magda said, shivering as she stared up at him. "Where are you going? Don't leave me!"

Caleb smiled at her. "I'll be back. Don't worry."

He strode to the mouth of the cave, his smile turning into a grin as his suspicions were confirmed. The moment he walked in, motion-sensing lights flickered on, and Caleb clapped his hands when he saw that Adam had equipped the room with everything a good Special Ops brother would need to get the fuck out of Dodge: Weapons ranging from knives and handguns to heavy artillery and even a goddamn spear; shelves full of fresh water and food rations (the good stuff, not the crap they actually give you in the military!); and, most importantly, clothes.

"What's your favorite color?" he yelled, his voice echoing off the walls of the cave. "Please say black, because that's all we've got."

Magda's voice came back, and Caleb realized she was walking towards him. "I like black," she said, a hint of excitement in her tone. "Ohmygod, this is like a . . . a . . . stash!"

"Stash is in fact the technical term for what this is," Caleb confirmed, pulling a set of waterproof black pants from the shelf along with a plain black t-shirt. He turned to Magda with the clothes, and almost fainted when he saw her standing there naked before him, her curves illuminated in the yellow light of the cave. "Oh, God," he groaned, feeling his cock harden inside his metal underwear to the point where

he wondered if he could just snap the lock with his
erection. "Oh, my God, Magda. You're . . . you're beautiful. So fucking beautiful."

"Stop saying that," she said softly, her arm covering her nipples, the other hand placed between her
legs, covering her feminine triangle. Even in the dim
light he could see she was blushing bright red, and everything in him wanted to scoop her up in his arms,
kiss her on those big red lips, show her that she was
his, now and forever. His woman, his mate, his goddamn witch!

"*You* stop saying that," he said, looking her in the
eyes and then letting his gaze move along her curves.
"How can you not know you're so gorgeous? Why
would you even want to hide this body?"

Magda frowned, a half smile breaking on her face.
She shook her head and sighed. "You don't know
what it's like to be teased as a girl, as a teen, as . . .
as a woman."

Caleb shrugged, still unable to tear his eyes away
from the sight of his mate, her curves looking smooth
and perfect, the elegant manner in which she was
covering her nipples and sex adding to his arousal in
a way that made his breath come in gasps. "Well, no.
Not as a woman," he said softly. "But I know what it's
like to be teased. Made fun of. Bullied." He grunted
as his face hardened, memories of his youth coming

through in flashes. "That didn't last long, though. Not when I found my Wolf. Found out who I was. What I was."

"You were teased as a kid? Bullied?" Magda said, frowning as her gaze moved up and down along his ripped, toned, tattooed soldier's body. "I don't believe that! What did the others kids say?"

Caleb grunted, turning away and holding out the clothes for Magda. "We were talking about you, not me. Here you go. I won't look. I promise."

He felt her take the clothes from him, and although everything in him wanted to turn and take in the sight of his mate in all her naked glory, he managed to hold firm and respect her privacy even though he thought it was ridiculous that a Shifter would feel ashamed of her natural body. Hell, he'd spent so much time naked that he wouldn't even *wear* clothes if not for the annoying rules of society! Not that he'd ever been interested in conforming to society, but whatever.

"You can look," came her voice, soft, trembling, unsure, but real.

Caleb felt his cock push against its metal cage as the blood rushed down from his head, making him sway on his feet. He grinned as he felt his wolf howl inside him, yelping like a horny teenager as it whipped around in frustration. But Caleb was actually enjoying the build-up, the restraint, the joyful misery of being held back from something he knew he was going to get eventually.

"No, it's OK," he said, trying to sound as nonchalant as possible. "I don't want to embarrass you. I'm a gentleman."

"Since when?" she teased.

"I've always been a gentleman," Caleb said, trying to make his voice sound regal and sophisticated. "That's how my father raised me. While he was getting drunk and throwing empty beer bottles at me for sport, of course. But he made a man out of me. A gentle-man, I mean."

"What? Really?" she said, her voice brimming with emotion in a way that sent a tremor through Caleb. Did she actually give a shit? Did someone actually give a shit about him? He could count on one hand the number of people who'd actually given a shit about him, and the realization that this woman, this mysterious creature who was dark witch and bashful teenager all in one was part of that select group made him want to howl out loud. "That's awful, Caleb! Where is your father now? I'll cast a spell on him! He'll be haunted by drunk ghosts for the rest of his days!"

"I don't know, and I don't care. He was gone the day after I Changed for the first time. Smart decision, because my wolf would have ripped him to shreds without hesitation. Hell, the boy I was would have done it too if I wasn't just a kid!"

Magda was quiet, and Caleb could hear her slipping into the pants and t-shirt. He sighed as he realized he'd missed his chance, ruined the moment by bringing up the worst part of his life, the worst person in his life.

"You would have killed your own father?" she said after a while. "Is that what we are when we're in animal form? Killers?"

Caleb snorted, folding his arms across his chest. "Humans are killers too, Magda." He sighed and slowly turned to face his mate. "But yes. Of course we're killers when Changed. Isn't that why you and Murad want an army of Shifters? Isn't that why I was training those misfits, trying to whip them into shape for . . . for what, exactly? I'm still not clear on what the hell you and Murad were planning to do with those beasts."

"I don't know if I'm so clear on it anymore either," Magda said softly, patting down the front of her t-shirt and reaching behind her to straighten out the pants that seemed wonderfully snug around her bottom. "How do I look?"

"Killer," said Caleb with a grin. "I can see the outline of your nipples through that shirt. Wow, they're big. May I just . . ."

Magda gasped in indignation, covering her boobs and raising her eyebrows. "I thought you were a gentleman!"

"I'll be gentle," Caleb said with a grin. "Just a quick

pinch. Perhaps a tweak. Just to make sure they're real."

"To make sure they're *real*? Are you accusing me of having fake boobs?"

"Who knows with you witches," said Caleb, his eyes flashing with mischief as he stared at the outlines of her big, beautiful globes pushing against the thin cloth of the military-issued t-shirt. "One moment you're a skinny, starved-out, twig of a woman, the next minute you're a voluptuous goddess that makes my cock so hard I can barely see straight."

Magda shrugged, raising her eyebrows and smiling as she hugged herself and turned sideways. "Well, you had your chance. Now you'll just have to wait."

Caleb tightened his jaw and took three swift steps towards his mate, going close to her and slipping his arm around her waist. He heard her gasp, felt her body tighten, smelled her scent rise up to him. He knew he was in control of this dance, and he loved it. He damned well loved it.

"You'll have to wait too," he whispered, bringing his lips close to hers, grazing her cheek as his right hand moved down along the small of her back, stopping just above the curve of her ass. He almost groaned out loud at the restraint it took to not squeeze her magnificent buttocks with both hands, squeeze them so hard she screamed. And then he'd pull those pants right down, flip her over his knee, spank the naughty witch until she released him from his spell. Hell yeah, that sounded good! What was he waiting for?!

"You're a tease," she whispered, her breath hot as she looked up at him. But he knew that *she* knew he was right. They both knew they had to wait. Jokes aside, Caleb couldn't forget that there was dark magic at play, that deals had been made in the past, that the dark powers were insidious, secretive, manipulative. They ebbed and flowed like the tides, retreating and advancing, using subterfuge and trickery to get their way. They were fated mates, yes—and certainly there was powerful magic involved there. But Caleb knew that the dark powers that lived inside his mate were part of this dance too. They *wanted* the two of them to mate. Which meant Caleb couldn't claim his mate until he fully understood why . . . why they wanted his first born child.

How the hell are we going to find out, though, Caleb thought as he held his mate close, heard her heart beat next to his, smelled the woman in her, the animal in her, his future in her. Does she even know?

"Do you?" he asked, completing his thought in words. "Do you know?"

"Do I know what?" she asked softly, nuzzling into him as he looked down at her. She looked so innocent with those rosy, full cheeks instead of the sunken cheekbones of a witch. Who was she, Caleb wondered. Which woman was real? Was he being played? Was *she* being played?

"Do you know who, why, what?" he said, feeling his mind start to kick into gear. He thought back to the early days when John Benson had recruited him out of Seal Team Nine, asking him if he was ready to serve his country, serve the world, serve all of mankind. Caleb was an American patriot down to the bone. He bled red, white, and blue, and he teared up every time he mouthed the words to the *Star Spangled Banner*. But he'd also been feeling restless as part of the Seals. Even in his small, close-knit team he'd felt like an outsider, a lone wolf, hiding from his own military brothers, hiding his true self. How the hell Benson had found out he was a wolf was anyone's guess, but Caleb was grateful for it. Benson gave him a chance to *be* his wolf, to let the Change come and go as the moon waxed and waned, to save the goddamn world along with a crew of beasts like himself, monsters living in the skin of men.

"Who, what, and why?" Magda repeated, looking up at him and scrunching her face up. "Am I being interrogated?"

"Trust me, babe," he said with a smile. "You'll know when you're being interrogated."

"Really? I thought the most effective interrogation happens when the subject doesn't know she's being interrogated."

"Exactly," said Caleb, his smile broadening to a grin. "Which is why I'm assuring you you're *not* being interrogated while I'm interrogating you. See what I'm doing?"

"Oh, the trickery," she murmured, resting her head against his chest as they stood there in the cave, witch and wolf, man and woman, fated mates facing their . . . fate? "You're such a good spy."

Caleb grunted. "Not really, though I was the most suited out of the three of us to be a spy. Adam's dragon was too full of rage and fire to handle finesse operations. And Bart the Bear . . . hah! No way was Butterball sneaking up on anyone! He was a battering ram!" He smiled, his heart suddenly filling with the most unbelievable warmth as he held Magda close. For one fleeting moment Caleb's life felt complete, full, overflowing with love and affection. He had a crew, a tribe, brothers in arms at his back. And here before him was his mate! Everything was laid out before him! A future he'd never imagined could be possible for a lone wolf!

But that future isn't here yet, Caleb reminded himself as that warmth quickly transformed into a chill when he looked down at Magda and thought he saw a flash of the witch in her. You're gonna have to fight for that future. Fight for your fate. Fight for your mate.

And then suddenly Caleb knew what he had to do.

"Where did it first happen?" he asked, frowning as he brushed a strand of hair from Magda's face.

"What?"

"You know what. The deal you made. The moment you allowed the dark power to enter you."

"It wasn't me," she said. "It was my animal. It was scared, terrified of being killed."

"Killed?" Caleb snorted. "No one can kill a Shifter's animal. You can kill a Shifter, sure. It ain't easy, but it can be done by another Shifter. But killing *just* the animal? I've never heard of that happening. Not even with magic."

"It wasn't magic," said Magda. "It was science. *Your* government's science."

Magda's words struck Caleb like a hammer, triggering a hazy memory from back when he and Bart the Bear had downed a couple beers (more like a couple dozen beers) and had a surprisingly deep conversation. The two Shifters had connected over the crap their own parents had subjected them to. Caleb had opened up about being insulted and assaulted as a boy too young to defend himself. And Bart had talked about how his parents, Bear Shifters themselves, had tried to "cure" him of his animal—of the Shifter "disease" as they called it. Cure him of his animal? Wasn't that just a nice way of saying "kill" his animal? Could it be . . .

The dots connected in Caleb's mind so fast he almost stumbled. American government scientists? Bart's parents? Could it be?

"How?" he said, his voice almost a whisper. "How did they find you? How did they know you were a Shifter?"

Magda shrugged. "They took me from my boarding school in Europe. I don't know how they knew I was a Shifter. It happened a few months after my first Change—at least the first Change that I remember."

"Where was the school?"

"In a small town in Germany," said Magda. "The middle of nowhere. On the fringes of the Black Forest. That's where I Changed for the first time."

Caleb's mind raced, the blood pounding in his temples as bits and pieces of his military knowledge came pouring in: snippets of conversations with Benson; patches of classified information from his time in Seal Team Nine; even conspiracy theories from the underground press and the goddamn *National Enquirer*!

"The U.S. military has a significant presence in Germany," he said, thinking aloud. "After World War Two we set up bases all over the country. And there've always been rumors that the Department of Defense likes to do its most controversial research outside the borders of the United States, just to maintain plausible deniability. There could be a secret research lab in the area near your school. Maybe they just . . . they just *saw* you, Magda. Pure coincidence. Sometimes the simplest explanation is the answer."

Magda nodded against his chest, but Caleb knew

that nothing was just coincidence when it came to this kind of shit. If there was a secret research facility near the Black Forest of Germany, there was reason it had been set up there.

And if there was anyone who'd know the reason, it was Benson.

John Benson.

"All right," said Caleb, his jaw tightening as he broke from the embrace and glanced around the cave. His gaze landed on a black rubber dinghy, and he grabbed it and began to drag it out to the water. It would take them about a day to get to the mainland from the island, and after that they'd have to find another means of transport to get to Abu Dhabi in the United Arab Emirates. Benson kept an office there, and even if he wasn't in town, Caleb would be able to contact him and get him to fly in.

"All right what?" said Magda. "Where are we going?"

"We're going to get to the bottom of this," he said. "Which means we need to go back to the beginning. To Ground Zero. Where it all began for you."

"The Black Forest?" Magda said, the color leaving her face so quickly she almost looked silver in the moonlight. But she wasn't scared, and in fact the look in her eye almost scared Caleb. He could see the dark power swirling behind her eyes as if this was exactly what that power wanted! Was he making a mistake? Would taking her back to the Black Forest only make the darkness in her more powerful?

"Yes," he said, swallowing hard and steeling his resolve. This was the way, he knew. There was a dark power that had a hold on his mate, and he would need to fight that power to free her. He would have to face that power and defeat it. That was his destiny. His calling. His goddamn fate.

"Yes," he said again. "The Black Forest. We just have to make a quick stop first. Conduct an interrogation."

12

ABU DHABI
UNITED ARAB EMIRATES

"**Y**ou aren't even going to waterboard me first?" said the distinguished, silver-haired man sitting calmly across the weathered teakwood desk. "I'm disappointed, Caleb. I thought I could at least turn *you* into a world-class spy. Getting a dragon and a bear in and out of a delicate situation without notice is impossible. But a wolf . . . now that was a promising experiment."

"Experiments," said Caleb, crossing his arms over

his broad chest and standing upright in front of the seated John Benson as Magda watched from the back of the room. "Funny you should use that word, John. Isn't it, honey?"

Benson frowned in a way that lit up his face, and Magda immediately felt like she could trust him. In fact she thought she could trust him more than she could trust herself! Over the past two days she'd been a woman in flux: Her fox had emerged; her body had reverted back to that curvy shape; the magic in her had receded as if it was being drained. But still she felt the dark power sitting there, crouching inside her like a shadowy presence like it was content to bide its time, like everything was flowing according to plan . . . according to *its* plan, not theirs!

"Honey?" Benson said, raising one bushy eyebrow and then the other. His light gray eyes twinkled as he looked at her and then stood up. "You two are mates? Hah! That's . . . that's wonderful, Caleb! Congratulations! The lone wolf finds his mate! Do Adam and Bart know?"

"Cut the crap, Benson," said Caleb, his voice sharp even as a smile curled the corners of his mouth. Magda could tell Caleb liked Benson, respected the man, even looked up to him. "Don't act so surprised. You always know what's going on."

Benson took a long breath and shook his head.

"Not this time," he said quietly, once again looking at Magda. "You're a Shifter?" he asked her politely, extending his hand in greeting.

"Yes," said Magda cordially, blinking and smiling as she shook his hand. "Fox."

A shadow passed across Benson's calm face, and Magda could tell that something had clicked in this se-cretive CIA-man's mind. He clearly hadn't recognized her by face, but hearing that she was a Fox-Shifter meant something to him.

"She's also a witch, John," said Caleb with a grin. "So be careful. She might turn you into a frog."

"Ribbit, ribbit," said Benson with a grin that looked authentic but was hiding something, Magda sensed. "I give up!"

All three of them laughed, but there was a tension in the air that Magda could almost see. Again she felt her dark powers swirl inside her like witch's brew simmering towards the boil, and Magda wondered if she should say something, warn them, let them know that if her dark powers were happily going along with what was happening, perhaps it was a trap.

"A Fox-Shifter and a witch, eh?" said Benson, ges-turing to the empty leather chairs in front of the desk before taking a seat himself. "Interesting mix."

"She's not a natural-born witch," said Caleb. "That's why we're here, Benson. We need answers."

But Benson's gaze hadn't moved from Magda, and

he narrowed his eyes and shook his head. "She *is* a natural-born witch," he said softly. "A Shifter-Witch. One of a kind. Isn't that right, Maggie? It is Maggie, isn't it? I'm glad to hear they didn't manage to kill your fox after all. I warned them it wouldn't work, but they tried anyway."

Magda stared as she felt a coldness run through her veins like ice water. She could feel the fox in her yelp and twist like it wanted to get out and run, run the hell away from here. And then she felt something else stir inside her, a power that lay at the bottom of it all, a power that had become tainted all those years ago, when her fox had invited the darkness into her, made a deal that had sent her down this path, a path that was leading her back to where it all began.

"You lying, manipulative sonofabitch," Caleb snarled, and Magda could see the hairs on his head and neck stand up straight. He was close to letting his wolf out, and Magda could sense the fear in Benson. John Benson was smart, yes. But he was still just human, and he had a healthy fear for a Shifter's animal. "I should rip your throat out right here and now."

"Hard for me to answer questions without a throat," said Benson, the sharpness of his tone masking the underlying fear. "Waterboarding is so much better." He laughed and winked at Magda. "I'm joking, of course. The U.S. government does not officially use torture of any form. Just like we don't run secret Department of Defense Research Labs in rural Germany, where we let our scientists experiment on Shifters for the advancement of the human race." He paused, taking a long breath as his gray eyes lost their sparkle and went deadly serious. "For the *survival* of the human race."

"Spare me the histrionic bullshit, John," growled Caleb, glancing at Magda and then back at Benson. "The biggest danger to the survival of the human race is other humans. And the U.S. Military is really good at killing bad humans. You don't need Shifters for that. In fact, the crew of Shifters you put together proved that it's too hard to control us. We screwed up that operation so bad even*you* couldn't save our asses!"

"That last part is true," said Benson. "But you're wrong about the rest of it."

"You mean the part about humans themselves being the biggest threat to the human race?" said Magda, frowning as she tried to remember if she'd ever met or seen Benson before. "You don't believe that?"

Benson slowly shook his head, rubbing his smooth chin as those gray eyes of his sunk deeper into shadow. "Not anymore," he said softly. "It's not so simple anymore."

"Murad," said Magda, her breath catching as she wondered if Benson knew that she was Murad's partner, that she'd been the one who'd helped Murad control his fearsome black dragon to the point where he was poised to do some real damage. "The Black Dragon."

But Benson just shook his head again. "Murad—which isn't his real name, by the way—is just a pawn in the bigger game. Just like you are, Maggie. Just like we *all* are." He took another slow breath, a tight smile emerging as he leaned back in his battered leather chair and put his feet up on the desk. "But like any chess player knows, a pawn in the right position can still win the game."

Caleb rubbed his buzzed head, his face twisting into a snarl. His wolf was riled up, itching to burst free, Magda could tell. She frowned as she tried to reach inside herself, call up her magic just in case she needed to stop him from Changing. Could she even do it? She'd been unsure of herself ever since that dinner party, when her fox had emerged and the witch seemed to have retreated. She'd tried to use her magic to transport her and Caleb to Abu Dhabi so they wouldn't have to drive all the way across the desert, but she'd been unable to get her spell to work. Would her magic work now? Would it ever work again? What was that comment about her being a natural-born witch? Sure didn't feel like it right now.

"You know I hate metaphors, John," Caleb snarled, leaning over the desk, his fingers gripping the wood so hard Magda wondered if his strength would splinter the heavy table. "Give it to me straight, or I swear to God I'll give it to *you* straight. Don't test me, John.

You know what I'm capable of. You know what my
animal is capable of."

Magda felt her dark power murmur in delight as
she watched her mate threaten his own mentor, and
in that moment she knew that a darkness lived inside
Caleb too. Was it "natural" or had she put it in him?
Was her *own* darkness natural or had it entered her
from the choices she and her fox had made years ago?
Suddenly she needed to know. She wanted to know.
She *yearned* to know.

"And you know what I'm capable of," she whispered,
her fingers curling up tight, her stomach knotting
up as she felt herself shrink inside her clothes. She
gasped as she felt her body morph once more into
the rail-thin frame of Magda the Witch, and from
the way Benson's eyes went wide, she could tell he
was as scared as a man who'd seen it all could ever be.

"Holy Mother of God," he whispered, pushing his
chair back from the desk and jumping to his feet. He
retreated against the far wall, blinking as his head
whipped from Magda to Caleb and then back to her.
"You're the dark witch! I have photographs of you
with Murad!"

"Wait," said Caleb, his snarl turning to a frown.
"You didn't know?"

Benson just shook his head. "No," he said hoarsely.

"But you just said you knew I was a witch," Magda
said. "You called me Maggie. You said I was a natural-born witch!"

"Yes, but a *good* witch," Benson said, his eyes still wide. "Your magic came from light, not darkness. What happened? What in the name of all that's holy happened, Maggie? What happened to you?!"

Magda felt dizzy as she tried to get her bearings. Her vision blurred, and she could feel her fox thrashing inside her, fighting to get out. That sick feeling of having no idea who she was, what she was, what she was meant to be came rushing back, and she almost doubled over in pain as she felt every part of her fighting to win, like there was a battle raging inside her, a battle that she couldn't possibly win without going insane!

But suddenly he was there, her mate, her man, her wolf. He was there, pulling her into his arms, pulling *all* of her into his arms: The witch, the animal, the woman. The dark and the light. The good and the bad. All of her. Every damned part of her splintered self.

And then he kissed her. By the demons of dark, by the angels of light, and by every power in between, he kissed her. Hell yes, he kissed her.

13

The kiss broke through her despair like the sun breaking through stormclouds, and Magda moaned as she felt a sudden balance whip through her convulsing body. Instantly she knew that the way out was through him, through her mate, through her fate, her destiny.

Him.

His touch.

His strength.

His love.

"What happened, Maggie?" came Benson's voice through the mist of the moment, and slowly Magda broke from the kiss as she remembered where they were, what was happening, what needed to happen . . . and what *had* happened: All those years ago in the Black Forest of Germany.

And so she talked, fast and furious, her memories pouring into speech that came out of her so fast she could barely breathe. She spoke of how she'd been that insecure girl, desperately looking for a source of strength, a way to fight back. And when she'd found it in her animal, they'd tried to kill her animal!

"And that's when I somehow got access to this dark magic," she said, blinking as she tried to remember the specific moment when it had happened. "But the magic was *always* dark. Nothing magical had ever happened before the experiments, when they tried to kill my animal and my fox made a deal with darkness. So I think you're wrong about me being a natural born witch."

"I'm rarely wrong," said Benson, shaking his head, his voice sounding confident once more. "Yes, there are things I don't know sometimes. But that's not the same as being wrong." He shook his head again, his eyes darting back and forth as if he was trying to think as fast as he could. "The Darkness can't just give someone powers out of thin air. It has to be based on something. You know that better than anyone, Magda. Or Maggie. May I call you Maggie?"

Magda blinked, feeling the fox inside nod yes, like being called Maggie lessened its frenzy. She nodded, feeling Caleb's warmth as he kept his arm tight around her waist, holding her close to his hard body. She frowned when she realized her hips were pressing against him, and then she gasped when she saw her curves were back. Maggie was back.

"Yes," she finally said, thinking back to how Bart the Bear and Bis the Leopard had opened themselves up to her dark magic by recognizing the darkness within themselves. That hadn't turned them into dark witches or wizards. It had simply built on whatever was already within them.

"The Darkness?" Caleb said, interrupting her thoughts. "You have a name for it?"

Benson shrugged. "You need to name something to gain power over it. Or at least to talk about it. The Darkness is as good a name as any."

"And so what is the Darkness? A demon?" said Caleb. "The Devil himself? Aliens?"

Benson snorted. "*Aliens*? Don't get me started on those assholes. That's a whole different mess I have to deal with."

Caleb's eyes went wide as he cocked his head. But then Magda saw the twinkle in Benson's eyes, and she burst into surprised laughter, setting off a cascade of snickers, giggles, and straight-up guffaws that broke through the madness and confusion for one delightful moment.

"Can I rip his throat out now, please?" Caleb muttered, his eyes narrowed to slits as his face relaxed into a big, beaming grin. "Holy crap, John. You had me going for a moment there!"

Benson winked. "Remember your training, soldier? The best time for a joke is when shit gets so crazy there's nothing to do but sit back and laugh."

Caleb nodded and grinned, and then he reached out his arm towards Benson, who gripped it tight in a military handshake that dated back to when men first banded together to face a common enemy. Magda smiled and shook her head, feeling the energy surge through her mate as he kept one hand tight around her waist, the other still locked tight with the old wardog Benson.

"Jokes aside," Benson finally said, still grinning with his gray eyes, "the answer to your question might just be *All of the Above*."

"What the hell are you talking about?" said Caleb.

"The Darkness," said Magda. "He's saying he doesn't know exactly what it is. It might as well be demons, the devil, and aliens all rolled up in one. He has no idea."

"Bullshit," said Caleb, breaking from the handshake and swiping at the air. "When John tells you he doesn't know something, you can bet your sweet ass he knows *exactly* what it is. This guy is *all* secrets, Magda."

Magda shook her head, feeling the balance of her

own powers flow through her in a way that was both serene and troubling, like the Darkness was just fine with what was happening here just like her fox seemed as relaxed as the hyperactive little critter had been since it had popped back from the dead.

"Not this time," she said, her gaze locked on Benson. "He doesn't know much about the Darkness because he knows enough to stay away from it. He knows that it will latch on to the darkness inside him and he'd never be able to break free. It would take over if he exposed himself to it. It would take him to a place from which he'd never return. He can't face it himself. He needs to send in his pawns. Us. You and me."

Caleb stared at Magda and then back at Benson. "What the hell is she talking about, John? What the hell are *you* talking about? When did you get all hokey and mystical on me? I thought you were a cold, calculating, logical bastard. Wheeling and dealing with dictators, terrorists, and everything in between."

"Exactly," said Benson, his gaze lingering on Magda like he was deeply affected by what she'd said. Finally he turned to Caleb. "I *am* a cold, calculating bastard, which means I know better than to enter into a game I can't win. I can't go up against this force I call the Darkness and expect to win." He let out a slow, trembling breath as he sank back into his chair and rubbed his chin. "But you two can. Together you two have a shot. It might be the only chance we have."

"Who is *we*?" said Caleb, his jaw still tight, blue eyes

riveted on the old CIA man who was clearly shaken in a way that was shaking Caleb himself. "You? The CIA? America?"

Benson grunted and shook his head. "This is way beyond that, Caleb. I already told you: This is about survival. Survival from extinction." He leaned forward on his scratched, weathered old teakwood desk, his face peaked, lips drawn out, gray eyes narrowed to slits. He looked at Magda and then back at Caleb. "This force, this thing called the Darkness, it . . . it doesn't have a body, it doesn't have a head, it can't be shot, stabbed, or blown up. It is energy, consciousness, pure dark emotion that infiltrates its victims from the inside out." He glanced at Magda, his eyes widening. "That is how dark magic works, isn't it? From the inside out? You gain its benefits by making a deal, by making a choice, by opening up to the darkness that already lives inside you, in your animal, in your human, by giving it room to grow, to breathe, to take over."

Magda nodded as she thought back once again to how the Darkness had entered her when she was a teenager. Little Maggie was *all* dark emotion back then, wasn't she? She hated everyone around her. She hated herself. Then her fox came out, and just when she saw a spark of light through the dark clouds that had surrounded her youth, those government scientists had taken her, taken her animal, leaving behind nothing but fear and more hatred. Hatred for every human around her. Hatred for *all* humans. Was that the essence of the Darkness? Hatred? Anger? Vengeance? The Holy Trinity of dark emotion?

"Why?" said Caleb. "Answer that question, John. Why?"

"I don't know," Benson said quietly. "But I have a theory."

Caleb snorted, shaking his head and glancing over at Magda, who was frowning hard as she tried to answer that question herself.

"He has a theory," Caleb whispered, rolling his eyes. "Here it comes, babe. Prepare yourself."

"Because the Darkness hates what it is not, what it can never be even though it yearns for it," whispered Magda as she felt the energy swirl inside her like a storm brewing. "And it can never live in the flesh, never experience three-dimensional life on Earth except through us. So it yearns to experience the joys of life in the flesh, but at the same time it *hates* that it yearns for that! So the result is hatred, frustration, anger. A need to corrupt, spoil, destroy. A need born out of . . . out of . . ."

"Conflict," said Benson, nodding as a grim smile emerged. "The draw of opposites, the need to seek unity, balance, equilibrium. It's a force at play everywhere in the universe: The way rivers flow to the ocean, the way air fills a vacuum, the way sound fills the silence. It's the same drive that makes men conquer new lands, trying to remake the world in their own image, spread their own beliefs, their own seed. And just like men have always wanted to be like the gods, sometimes the gods yearn to be human even though they don't want to give up the power that comes from *not*being human. Just like a child wants the toy that it *doesn't* have!"

Caleb took a sharp breath, his grip around Magda's waist tightening as she sensed his frustration. "This isn't helping clear things up," he grumbled, rubbing his head with his free hand. "What's the end game here, John?"

Benson just smiled and shook his head. "There is no end game. It's all just one game. One dance. The eternal dance of the universe. Back and forth, in and out, up and down. Right now the Darkness is on the upswing. Look at what's happening in the world. There is more misery, war, and injustice now than ever before! But like the saying goes, *Life will find a way*. And it has." He glanced at Magda and then back at Caleb. "With you two. With Adam and Ash. Bart and Bis. And all the Shifters who are waking up to their destinies, to their futures, to their fate."

"Life will find a way," Caleb said slowly. "Did you seriously just quote a line from *Jurassic Park*?"

"Don't interrupt my inspirational speech, Soldier," said Benson with a twinkle in his eye. "My point is that the universe itself is always seeking balance,

which means that as the Darkness rises, we can expect an opposing force to rise along with it. I've spent
decades wondering exactly *what* that force is going
to be, and now I see it. I see it standing before me."
He paused, and Magda swore she saw his lips tremble with emotion, his eyes misting up until he quickly blinked and looked away as if he was embarrassed.
"Love in its purest form. One-on-one love ordained by
the universe. Love that forces two creatures of flesh-
and-blood to overcome all conflict, to merge their opposites, to find a way to the promised land, back to
the Garden of Eden, to their own happily ever after."

"Holy Mother of God, he's lost it," Caleb muttered,
shaking his head. "He's finally cracked. Too many
years of sitting in safehouses and listening to violent
madmen speak about their visions of the world. Or
maybe he's just been sitting alone in the dark read-
ing romance novels on his Kindle. Fifty-fifty shot
on either of those options. Let's go before he starts
bawling. I don't think I can handle that."

But Magda reached her arm around Caleb and dug
her fingers in tight as she felt her fox move inside her,
sensed her mate's wolf move inside him. Their animals were listening too, and they were agreeing with
Benson. He was right. Wasn't every Shifter faced with
the challenge of balancing their animal with their human? Wasn't every Shifter faced with the unstoppable draw towards their fated mate, forced to confront

every obstacle that comes between them and their union? The story of the Shifter was the story of life in its purest form, wasn't it? How do you balance the needs of the flesh with the needs of the spirit? How do you balance the dark and the light? The man and the woman? The animal and the human? The need to kill with the need to create new life?

She looked over at Caleb. Caleb the Soldier. Caleb the Wolf. Caleb the Man. Caleb the Shifter. Caleb her mate. Then she closed her eyes and turned her gaze inward, her body trembling as she saw the opposites that made her who she was: Witch, fox, woman, angry teenager. The ambition to rule the world mixing with the drive to give birth, to cuddle her pups, to bear more children for her mate. The needs of her fox to run wild, to hunt, to mate . . . to just *be*.

Slowly she opened her eyes and nodded. "You're saying that Shifters are the universe's response to the growing power of the Darkness. Shifters coming together with their fated mates is the force that can counter the Darkness, because it's the purest form of love, a love that serves the needs of the animal and the human, the body and the spirit, the darkness and the light."

Caleb let out a massive sigh. "Finally! Now *that* I can understand! I coulda told you that the first time we kissed. Man! All this pointless babbling, and all we needed to do is get down to it and just fu—"

Magda felt herself go flush with embarrassment as she dug her fingers hard into his side. She could feel her fox yelping in glee, turning round and round inside her so fast she got an image of a red spinning furball, its heat rising for its mate. But still she could sense that darkness sitting there in the background, cold and silent, watching and waiting, like this was all still playing out exactly the way it wanted.

"It's not that simple," she finally said. "And you know it, Caleb. We can't . . . we can't do *that* until . . ."

Caleb went quiet, and Magda knew he was thinking about what she'd told him earlier, in private, about the deal she'd made all those years ago. Her first born child. Was it real? Or was the deal just part of her imagination, something that a bookish teenager had pulled from a scary story. Hell, it was the oldest story in the book, wasn't it? The demon or dark power asking for the first born child! Maybe she'd just made it up! Made up the whole thing with the deal!

"Well," said Benson, clearing his throat as if he was uncomfortable talking about matters this personal, "whatever you two need to work out, I'd suggest you get started." He glanced at Magda, his face grim as he reached for a phone and tapped on the screen. He turned the phone around so they could see the video that had started to play, and Magda gasped when she focused on the screen.

It was the Black Dragon, Murad, flying across the

desert, massive wings spread out wide, golden eyes burning like dark flame. The video had been taken via satellite, and below the wings of the dragon Magda could see hundred of Shifters, beasts in animal form, all of them bounding across the burning sand of the desert like they were on a mission.

"What the hell," Caleb muttered, leaning forward and grabbing the phone. "That's Darius the Lion Shifter at the helm. Everett the Tiger Shifter bringing up the rear. How the hell did Murad get all those wild animals to actually . . ." He trailed off, blinking hard as he rubbed his stubble and glanced over at Magda. "This is not good. This is very, very not good. Where is this? When was this? Where the hell are they going?"

"Swipe to the next video," Benson said softly, rubbing his forehead. "This was last night."

"Motherfu—" Caleb shouted, ripping away from Magda and stomping through the room, growling and snorting as if he was trying to hold his wolf back from bursting forth. "No way. No *way*! I did this, John! I trained those beasts! What did I do! What the fuck did I *do*?!"

"We both did it," Magda said quietly, feeling her darkness slither through her like a snake tightening its coils around her insides, reminding her that it was still there, deep inside her, taking hold, never coming out. She stared back at the video of Murad's Black

Dragon leading its army of feral Shifters into battle.

Of course, it wasn't a battle.

It was a massacre.

A night raid on a small village in Western Iraq. A practice run for Murad's army. Just stretching their legs. Sharpening their claws. Bloodying their teeth. Giving the animals a taste of what was to come: Death, destruction, chaos. The Apocalypse, the Darkness, the end of the world—whatever name you wanted to give it. It was coming, and she and her mate were the only things standing in the way right now.

"Why us?" she said suddenly, her eyes still riveted on the footage of Murad's Black Dragon ripping through sandstone houses like they were made of canvas, burning men, women, children, and pets alike, swallowing some whole, tossing a few to his savage Shifters, who ripped them apart like feral beasts fighting over scraps. "You said you think the counter-force to the Darkness is Shifters waking up and finding their mates, restoring balance to the world we're living in. So that's much bigger than us, isn't it?" She looked at the feral Shifters on the screen, led by the rampaging Black Dragon, the one she'd held in check for years with her magic . . . magic that she wasn't sure would ever be powerful enough to stop him again.

Not unless . . . she started to think as she felt the darkness in her nod like it was a living, breathing thing of the night. Not unless you make a sacrifice.

You want the power to stop Murad's dragon now that it's been unleashed? Then you need to take the Darkness further into your soul. *That's* why the deal for a first-born child is the oldest deal in the history of darkness! It's not about the child itself; it's about what it means to give up what's most precious to a creature of flesh and blood, what's most precious to a mother. Making a choice like that takes you to a dark place from which there's no coming back.

Absolute darkness.

Absolute power.

It's a paradox, Magda realized as she felt her fox scream inside her like even its sly intelligence was no match for the insidiousness of the Darkness. That's how darkness works, isn't it? Forces you to make an impossible choice, a choice where you lose either way! I'm being offered a chance to save the world from Murad's Black Dragon, but in return I'll have to give up what's most precious to me, give up *my* world! I can't win!

Not alone, no, came her fox's whisper after a moment of silence. *But with him you can. Together you can. You and him. All of us together.*

"Why me?" she said again, suddenly furious for being in this position, wondering if she was going crazy.

"Because you're special, Magda," said Benson softly. "A witch Shifter. Natural born witch, and natural born Shifter. Once you manage to accept and balance all the parts of yourself, you'll gain access to power that can put the Black Dragon back inside Murad and hold it there."

"I told you already, I'm *not* a natural born witch!" Magda screamed, pulling at her hair as she began to pace the room. She could feel her body expanding and contracting with each heated breath, like she was morphing back and forth between the witch and the woman even as her fox twisted into a cowering fur-ball inside her. "My magic came from the Darkness, and even then it was barely enough to hold Murad's dragon in check all these years. To gain the kind of power to put the Black Dragon back into the Sheikh means I'll have to go deeper into the Darkness, maybe*all* the way!"

"OK, timeout!" Caleb shouted, stepping in and trying to grab Magda as she clawed at her hair, not sure if her witch or her fox was going to burst forth first. "Nobody's going anywhere—not yet, at least." He turned to Benson. "John, if what you're saying about Shifters and their fated mates is true, then if Murad finds *his* fated mate, that should stop his rampage, shouldn't it?"

Benson sighed and closed his eyes. He pressed his hands together like he was trying to meditate or something, and after a long moment he opened his eyes and exhaled. "That's the problem," he whispered. "Murad *did* find his fated mate. He found her, and he killed her. There's no coming back from that. He is all dark. All self-hatred. All beast. He will never find balance."

"Then we just kill him," Caleb said, his jaw tightening as he finally got a hold of Magda and pulled her into his hard body. "We're the goddamn United States Military, John. We can kill anything a hundred times over. We just kill him. Poof. Done."

Benson snorted. "You know as well as I do that the only thing that can kill a dragon is another dragon. And there's only one other dragon that I know of."

"Adam," said Caleb, his face going pale as Magda watched her mate connect the dots in his head. "Oh, shit, John. You're saying if Magda can't put the Black Dragon back into the bottle, the only other option is for . . . is to have Adam . . ."

"Kill his own father," Magda said, a tight smile of pure ice coming across her face as she felt the Darkness tremble with laughter, shiver with glee, rub its invisible hands together in pure delight at the masterful game of manipulation it was unleashing. Now they were *all* in it, weren't they?

"If it's too late to save Murad," Caleb said slowly, "then Adam will kill him if that's what it takes to stop what's happening. You know he will."

"Yes," said Benson, his face still grim. "But then what happens? Think about it! What would it do to Adam to take the life of his own father? What would it do to his heart, his soul, his own dragon?"

"Shit," said Caleb, rubbing his forehead and shaking his head. "You're right. It might turn Adam's dragon all dark. Killing one dark dragon might just unleash another one! Which means . . ." he started to say, looking down at Magda as the realization showed on his taut, lean face.

Magda nodded, closing her eyes as she kept that cold smile on her lips. Benson was right. This *was* up to her and her mate. Yes, the longer game was for Shifters around the world to wake up and start finding their mates. But the immediate need was to stop Murad's Black Dragon from its rampage or else there wouldn't *be* a world! The War for Balance would continue as every Shifter out there found its mate; but this first battle had to be won now.

"All right," she said, her eyes flashing as she studied Benson's expression. Yes, this was a man of secrets, with his own darkness. But he had accepted his darkness, accepted that he'd done what he needed to do over the course of his life, made compromises and sacrifices for the greater good. Now she and Caleb would have to do the same. "I still don't believe I'm a natural born witch, though."

"You will when you go back there," Benson said softly. "Back to where it all began for you. How did you end up at an obscure boarding school for girls nestled in Germany's Black Forest, Magda? Why is the Darkness so strong in that part of the world? Why did the

U.S. Military set up a secret facility for Paranormal Research right there? Did you know that Hitler and the major figures of the Third Reich were deeply interested in the occult and paranormal? So were the Russians during the height of the Cold War. And so are we. The War for Balance is bigger than the two of you, yes. But this battle is all on you. I'll work with Adam and Bart to see if we can slow Murad's army down to give you some time."

"Some time for what?" Caleb said, agitation in his voice even though Magda could feel his heart beating steady like a soldier's, firm and focused like a man with a mission.

Benson grinned, shrugging and then winking at Caleb. "To save the fucking world, Soldier. You in?"

Caleb's eyes went wide, and then he just shouted with laughter tinged with a madness that Magda could feel in herself too. She needed him, she knew. She needed him by her side as she dug into her own past, confronted her own demons, fought her internal battle as the battle outside raged on.

And somewhere along this journey he's going to need me too, she realized as she saw the midnight blue in his eyes and remembered that there was so much about this man that was still a mystery to her. She knew he was her mate, but that was it. She didn't really know where he came from, where he was going, what demons lived inside him, what darkness lay hiding there beside his inner wolf.

"You know I'm in," said Caleb, his wolf speaking through the man in a way that made Magda shiver. "In it to win it, baby. Now and forever. Ow, ow, owwwooooo!"

14

"**O**w!" snarled Caleb, frowning down at his metal underwear as he examined the padlock. "Why is this still on me, may I ask?"

"You know why," Magda said, turning her head toward him as she led the way. "I don't trust you. I don't trust myself. And I certainly don't trust our animals. Besides, I think you're stuck with it. I don't think I have access to my magic any longer."

"Liar," said Caleb, stomping over twigs and fallen branches as he followed his curvy mate into the depths of Germany's mountainous Black Forest region. Benson had gotten an unmarked plane to fly them west past Russia and Poland to Germany, dropping them off as close to the Black Forest as possible. "I saw you conjure up those clothes you're wearing."

"You like them?" Magda said cheekily, twirling around as she walked so her long white gown rose up just enough to give him a glimpse of her beautifully formed thighs. "I designed it myself, you know."

"No wonder it covers up so much," Caleb muttered. "Next time let me design your clothes." He looked down at his underwear again, knocking on the metal. "I'd also like to design my own clothes, actually."

"And by that do you mean no clothes at all?"

Caleb shrugged. "Animals don't wear clothes. And neither should witches, in my opinion. Especially witches with curves like that. Twirl once more for me, please."

"No," said Magda, laughing as she shook her head and stepped up the pace. "You don't tell me what to do. Remember, I'm the witch and you're my familiar."

"Exactly," Caleb growled, taking three quick steps and grabbing her around the waist. He twirled her around so fast she gasped, and he drew close and sniffed her neck as his wolf howled for him to get a move on with what they all knew had to happen, was meant to happen, *needed* to happen! "And I need to get more familiar with your body, Witch. It's time, Magda. Don't make me wait any longer. I can smell your little fox inside. It's in heat, just like my big, bad wolf."

"Your big bad wolf?" Magda whispered, looking up

into his eyes as he held her by the waist. "Am I Red Riding Hood in this story now? What happened to the wicked witch?"

"The only wickedness I've seen from you lately is this medieval suit that's suffocating my cock," Caleb grumbled, releasing her from his grip and pushing her away sulkily. "Though you know it can't hold my wolf back. I can Change and rip through this like it's a paper bag."

"I know. I've seen you do it," Magda said, straightening out her gown, her bosom moving in the most divinely arousing way as she tried to slow down her breathing. Caleb could see she was aroused, that her animal could sense his animal's heat, that the woman in the witch wanted the man standing before her. But still they were playing this game. Still there was something holding them back, just like there was something urging them on. "But you said it yourself: Shifters can't mate while in animal form. And when you Change back, your little cage reappears like magic."

"Call me little again," Caleb snarled. "Go on. I dare you."

"Is that a threat? I don't think it's wise to threaten a wicked witch."

"I'm not known for my wisdom," Caleb grunted, sighing as he followed Magda along a mountainous path through the thickly wooded Black Forest. He took a deep breath, feeling the energy of the woods enter his body along with a million different scents, sounds, and colors. He could feel his wolf eagerly sniffing too, like it was delighted to be out in the wild, the peacefulness of the forest taking the edge off its stymied arousal.

"What are you known for?" Magda asked, half-serious as she carefully stepped between two jagged rocks in her completely inappropriate shoes. "Ow. Shit. Why didn't I conjure myself some hiking boots instead of these red pumps?"

"Aha! So you admit that you still have access to your magic!" Caleb said. "And you also admit that you suck at designing clothes."

"My clothes are fine for the weather. As for my shoes . . . well, just like a man doesn't like to be called little, a woman doesn't like any negative comments about her shoes."

"Is *that* a threat?" Caleb said, grinning as he leaned forward and smacked her playfully on the butt as she bent down to get a pebble out from her shoe. "*Bad* witch!"

"Ouch!" she squealed, standing up abruptly and turning to him, her face red with shock. "That hurt!"

"I barely touched you, witch. And I got you right on the meaty part of your butt, so I know it didn't actually hurt. I know what I'm doing."

"What the hell does that mean?" Magda said, putting her hands on her hips, her eyes going wide. "Did you call me fat while boasting about your sexual prowess all in the same sentence?!"

"Actually it was several sentences," Caleb said, his wolfish grin growing as he imagined his finger marks on her ass. Then he felt his cock clang against the inside of his metal cage like it was banging to get out, and he just shook his head when he realized he was loving this slow build to what he knew was coming. "And I didn't call you fat, I called you meaty. As for boasting about my sexual prowess . . . well, why is a playful smack on your butt sexual? That's a clear indication that you've got sex on your mind, you bad, *bad* witch."

"OK, *meaty* is even worse than fat. What am I, a lamb chop?" Magda said, scrunching her face up as she glanced back at him, her eyes brown and big, so far removed from those dark slits of the "other" witch that Caleb felt a chill go through him as he wondered if they were being lured into a trap.

He looked around, breathing deep once again, closing his eyes as he let his inner wolf take in all the sensations of the forest. His wolf had an almost otherworldly sense for impending danger, and Caleb stayed silent as he let his beast do what it did best.

But the wolf was calm, controlled, happy even, and so Caleb exhaled and kept walking behind his mate, doing his best to keep his eyes off her big, beautiful butt. It wasn't easy, and finally he gave up and just stared shamelessly as her rear globes moved sublimely beneath her white gown. He wanted to push her face down, lift up that dress, spread her thighs and cheeks and lick her until his wolf howled to the moon, until her fox yelped in its frenzy, until his witch wailed to be taken, claimed, mated, straight-up fucked.

Suddenly a shadow passed over the sun-bathed green forest, and Caleb frowned as he looked to see whether some cloud cover had arrived. Nope. Still blue sky and burning sun. The forest was getting thicker, denser, more wooded as they kept walking, but Caleb was certain it had been a moving shadow. Another animal, perhaps? This was the forest, after all. He'd picked up the scent of a hundred different animals already: everything from hares, rabbits, and squirrels to snakes, wild boar, and the German variation on the mountain lion.

He wasn't afraid of some mountain lion, of course. His wolf could hold its own against any beast of the wild, and most certainly a big cat would have smelled Caleb's wolf and kept its distance anyway. But the thought reminded him of that video Benson had shown them back in Abu Dhabi: That scene of Murad's Black Dragon leading an army of Shifters . . . an army that Caleb had trained! Darius the Lion Shifter leading the ground forces. Everett the Tiger bringing up the rear guard. Both those big cats had been wild and uncontrollable when they'd been put under Caleb's watch, but clearly they had fallen in line now—or at least some semblance of it.

Caleb's jaw tightened as he realized he'd have to face them at some point. Face those big-cat Shifters on the battlefield. He might have to kill them, and the thought stuck like a dagger in his heart. Only then did he realize that during those months of corralling a group of immature, almost feral Shifters, he'd actually grown attached to them, actually begun to care about them, actually thought of them as his crewmates. Not in the same way that Adam and Bart were his crew, of course—not yet, at least.

Adam and Bart aren't just my crew, Caleb reminded himself as he felt a glow of warmth inside him. They're my family. My pack. All of them.

An image of Bart and Bis's kids came to him as he absentmindedly kept staring at Magda's rear as she climbed up the steep mountain path in front of him. He remembered how he'd felt when he'd asked to see their cubs while they were still at Murad's castle. He remembered that strange yearning he'd felt when he saw the helpless babes reach for their mother, giggle at their father, crying out for love and attention—*insisting* on being loved and attended to! His mind moved on to the memory of Adam and Ash's kids when they were captured, and he remembered how although he'd kidnapped them, he was certain he'd never be able to harm one hair on their fuzzy little heads.

He grinned as the thoughts made his wolf rumble inside him, like it was enjoying the emotions that were rolling through the human. Soon Caleb's grin was so wide he almost cried out in delight. Shit, a moment ago he was fantasizing about spanking his mate's ass and taking her hard and quick right here in the middle of the forest. And now he was fantasizing about having babies with her, raising children together, being a dad to little fox-wolf critters of mixed blood! Being a father! A freakin' *father*!

"Was your father always a violent drunk or did you two actually get along at some point?" came Magda's voice through Caleb's daydream, and the question fit in so perfectly with his thoughts that Caleb almost choked as he wondered if he'd been thinking aloud.

"Why . . . why would you ask me that out of the blue?" he said, frowning as he reminded himself that she was a witch, that they were heading back to the place where she'd first gotten access to her dark magic, that this force Benson called the Darkness was watching them, waiting for them . . . was perhaps *in* them!

Magda shrugged, her back still turned to him as she picked up the pace like they were getting close to their destination—whatever that was.

"I don't know," she said. "Just making conversation. You'd gone quiet suddenly, and I was wondering what you were thinking about."

"Then why not just ask me what I was thinking about instead of ambushing me with a question like that?" Caleb snapped, not sure why his mood had suddenly darkened when a moment ago he had almost burst into song, he was so happy!

"How is asking you about your father an *ambush*?" Magda said, her own voice sharp with the rebuttal. "Does the big, bad wolf have daddy issues?"

Caleb snarled as he felt his wolf bare its fangs inside him. It wanted to come out, and as Caleb held back the Change, it occurred to him that it was really strange that they'd been making this long trek through the forest in human form when it would be so much simpler as animals. He frowned hard as he tried to ignore Magda's jab, but he could feel his anger rising, his wolf growling, his toes curling, his fists clenching. Her tone had been sharp, not playful like it had been before. Perhaps he was imagining it, but it seemed like she was enjoying riling him up, sticking a knife in him and twisting. What had happened suddenly?!

Again he caught movement in his peripheral vision, a shadow passing through the dark forest around them. Now he was on high alert, his eyes wide, his wolf close to bursting forth. What the hell was happening? Was this the Darkness at play? What was its game? What did it want? Did it want them to fight? Or did it want them to . . .

Caleb looked down at his metal underwear, frowning again as he thought about how it had started as a joke but was now a real thing. Hell, he'd have taken her a hundred times by now if not for this metal thing that would shatter when he Changed to wolf form but popped back onto him when he Changed back to the man. Yes, he'd have taken her, and she'd be pregnant with a goddamn litter of his wolf-pups!

"What about *your* parents?" he asked quickly, trying to ignore questions he couldn't answer: question about himself, questions about what was happening here—shit, what the hell were they even *doing* here! There was a war coming, Adam and Bart were going to be in the middle of it, and he was on a goddamn hiking trip in Germany with a chastity belt on?! How did this make any sense?!

It will all make sense in a moment, whispered his wolf, its inner voice sounding strangely calm given how riled up Caleb the man was. *We are almost there.*

Where, Caleb replied angrily in his head. And how the hell do *you* know where we're going when I don't?

Because I have been here before, whispered his wolf. *I remember all of it.*

"Bullshit," Caleb muttered under his breath. He looked around, taking in the sight of the mountain peaks above them, the heavily wooded lowlands of the Black Forest beneath them. "We've never been here before. I'd remember by now."

I didn't say we, replied his wolf in that same calm, cold voice. *I said I've been here. Not we. I. Just me. Me without you. The wolf without the human. I came face to face with it. I faced it when you couldn't. I faced it for you, to save you, to save us both. Just like her fox did what it needed to do, your wolf did what had to be done.*

15

"**W**hat the *hell* are you talking about?" Caleb roared from behind Magda, and she stopped in her tracks and turned to him, her eyes wide when she heard the edge in his voice.

"What?" she said, stammering as she looked into his eyes that had turned ice-blue. It took a moment for her to realize he was talking to his wolf, not to her. "What's going on, Caleb? What's your animal saying?"

Caleb was rubbing his buzzed head and stomping about like he was trying to put out a fire, and it took a moment for him to even acknowledge her presence, he was so busy yelling at his wolf, calling it a liar, cursing it up and down like he'd gone insane.

"It's saying it's been here before," he finally muttered through gritted teeth.

Magda frowned as she stared at Caleb and then around at the trees. "Here? You've been to these woods before? When?"

"Never. That's the goddamn point, Magda. My wolf is saying that it was here without me! The wolf without the man! That's not possible! That's just not *possible!*"

It is possible, whispered Magda's fox from inside her. Her animal had been quiet for days, and its voice startled her.

"What do you mean?" she asked her animal, not bothering to keep her voice down. Caleb was still ranting and raving at his animal, and so she might as well get into it with her fox.

The wolf was indeed here without the man, because at the time there was no man. There was just a boy. An angry boy full of rage, full of hate, full of fury but too small and weak to do anything.

"To do anything about what?" Magda demanded, noticing for the first time that the forest around them had turned dark even though the sun was shining above the tree cover. She thought she saw shadows moving around them, as if the trees themselves were moving in a way that trees shouldn't move. But she ignored it, focusing on her animal, prodding it for answers. "Too small and weak to do anything about *what*?" she screamed as the trees around her began to thrash even though the air was dead around them.

"My father!" howled Caleb from beside her, his hands clawing at his head as he stumbled around like he was drunk. "I killed him, Magda! I killed him before he had a chance to kill my mother. To kill me. I fucking *killed* him!"

16

Correction, whispered Caleb's wolf, its voice still calm and controlled. *I killed him. You were too young to even stand on your own, let alone fight a grown Wolf Shifter like your father. You were still decades away from your first Change, and although I wanted to come forth to protect your mother and you, I knew that if a transformation happens before the human is ready, it could kill him, kill both of us.*

"But you *did* come forth!" Caleb shouted as the memories rolled back through him like an avalanche. Snippets of scenes from his childhood: His father, a massive Wolf Shifter who'd never truly gained control over his animal, over his human, over his need for drink, drugs, violence. Terrorizing his own family was sport to him, and Caleb shouted again as he tried to block out those images of his father Changing back and forth in a drunken rage, beating his mother one moment, biting his son the next, clawing at his own mate until she screamed as blood poured from her shredded skin, slashing at his own son until his arms and legs looked like they'd been decorated with blood-red ribbons. "You *did* come forth! I remember it! I Changed and we killed the monster together."

No, said his wolf. *Think back, Caleb. That was not your true first transformation. You had not Changed. You were still a boy, frozen in place, watching the wolf inside you burst out and do what you could not. Think about it: After that night, when was the next time you Changed?*

Caleb blinked as he searched his memories. Shit, his wolf was right. The next time he'd Changed was decades later, when he'd already joined the military. He'd had dreams, visions, flashbacks throughout his teenage years, images of himself in wolf form, an animal roaming free through the woods. But the first Change since the day his wolf had killed his father was indeed decades later, on a full-moon night out on the ocean, during the phase of training that tested a Seal to his limits: One night afloat on the dark ocean. All alone. Always alone.

Caleb stared at Magda as his wolf sat there in the background as if it was waiting for something. She was screaming at her fox, he could tell. What the hell was it saying to her?

It is telling her that it is time, his wolf whispered. *Her fox ventured into these same woods to ask for the power of the Darkness. I did that too. We both made deals with the Darkness, and that is why we are still alive to tell the tale. That is also why we have led you two back here. Because it is time.*

"The Darkness," Caleb muttered, staring wide-eyed as the trees swayed even though there was no wind. "You know what it is?"

Yes, answered his wolf after a long moment. *Every Shifter's animal knows what the Darkness is. It is the source of the animal's power. It is the essence of the Shifter spirit, distilled over eons, animal energy in its purest, most refined, most perfect form. Pure carnal energy. It is the Darkness that drives the Shifter's animal to kill, to feed, to run rampage.*

"What the hell are you saying?" Caleb muttered, watching Magda talk to her fox as if it was telling her the same thing, as if their two animals had engineered all of this and were now saying, *Haha! Fooled ya! Wouldn't like to be ya!*

"What the hell are you saying?!" Caleb said again, his voice rising this time. "You're saying every Shifter's animal is inherently . . . *evil*? I can't believe that! I *won't* believe that!"

Good and evil are inventions of humans, said his wolf

matter-of-factly. *Please leave the animals out of it. The Darkness is neither good nor evil. It just . . . is.*

"It just *is*?! That's your answer?!" Caleb roared, punching a tree-trunk so hard he knew he'd have some serious bruises in a few hours. "Not good enough, you goddamned furball. *Not! Good! Enough!*"

"Caleb!" Magda screamed, flinging herself into his body so hard it almost knocked the wind out of him. But he grabbed her and pulled her in close, looking upon her tear-streaked face that made it clear her fox had just told her exactly what his wolf had just revealed. "Caleb, what is your animal telling you? Don't listen to it, Caleb! It's a trick! We can't trust our animals right now! Not here! Not in this place!"

Caleb frowned as he felt his mind squirm like a toad in the sun. Suddenly there were too many people talking at once, too many voices in his head, too many sounds from the trees, too much, too much, just too damned much!

Take her, whispered his wolf through the chaos. *You want answers? You want to know what the Darkness is? You want to see it, touch it, face it dead on like a soldier? Then draw it out into the open. Give it what it wants. Give it what it has been promised. Give it what it wants, and it will come for it. Take her now, Caleb. Claim your mate. Her fox is blocking her dark magic, and she will not be able to stop you. Take control. Take your mate. Claim your fate.*

A strange peace came over Caleb, but it was the eerie peace of a desert island before a hurricane comes screaming in. He could feel the energy building up in his core, and as his mind cleared out all the voices, Caleb was certain he understood what the wolf was talking about when he said the Darkness was the source of every Shifter's animal energy. Wasn't it true that without balance and control a Shifter's animal was a destructive, merciless, ruthless force? Look at Adam's dragon when it went on a rampage! Look at Bart's bear when it was out of control! Those beasts killed without discrimination! No prisoners! No survivors! No leftovers for the morning!

I'm a goddamn killer too, Caleb reminded himself as he tightened his grip around his mate and looked deep into her eyes. And so is she. So is my mate. My woman. My witch.

That one look at her eyes told him that her mind was swirling too, that she was turned around inside, twisted and torn as to whether this was magic or madness, real or imagined, the path to their destiny or the road to eternal darkness.

Give it what it wants and it will come for it, his animal had whispered as Caleb cocked his head and let his gaze move down along Magda's bosom overflowing past her white gown's neckline. That's what you want, isn't it, Soldier? To face your enemy on the battlefield? To draw it out into the open?

"Yes," Caleb whispered, leaning close and slowly licking Magda's neck as she swooned in his arms, shivered at his touch, and finally let out a low moan that made Caleb tremble. He could feel his manhood push against the metal lock like it had before, but this time he swore he could feel the metal begin to bend under his power, from his need, his need to fill her with his seed. "Yes, that's the answer. All this while we've been trying to hold ourselves back from doing what comes naturally, and we've been restraining ourselves out of fear. But I'm a goddamn soldier. I face my fears. I fight my fears. I *kill* my fears."

"What are you talking about?" Magda mumbled, her eyelids fluttering like she was under a spell—or perhaps just coming out of a spell.

"The Darkness wants our first born, right? Well, then let's give it what it wants. Bring it out into the open. I want to see this mysterious force called the Darkness. I want to face it. Let's see if it can take my child from me. My baby from me. *Anything* from me! We're going to finish this before we leave this forest, Magda. *I'm* going to finish this. Kill the enemy and walk out of here with my woman and my baby."

"No!" Magda shrieked as she tried to get away from him. "No, Caleb! You don't understand! We need to . . . oh, God, Caleb. Oh, *God*!"

And then Caleb couldn't hear her voice, couldn't see her face, couldn't even breathe. Because he'd leaned in and kissed her. He'd kissed her hard, and his mouth smothered hers as he felt his wolf howl, sensed her fox yelp, smelled her feminine musk rise up to him like a drug in the thick, heavy air of the dark forest.

He kissed her. By the eternal Darkness that lives in every Shifter, he kissed her.

17

His kiss broke her down the middle, shattered her from the inside out, sent sparks through her body, tremors through her soul. She could hear his wolf's howl rip through the ether, her fox yipping and yelping in unison as it gave itself up to its powerful, dominant mate. She could sense her animal had been waiting its entire life for this moment, perhaps while dreading the day it happened, knowing what was promised.

The memory of that promise almost broke her in two again, and she tried to break away from his kiss. But she couldn't. He was too strong, and when she felt his rock-hard manhood pushing against her thighs and force them apart, she realized that the barrier she'd managed to keep up to control their cravings for one another was now gone.

Magda tried to conjure up that metal cage again, almost panicking when she realized her magic wasn't working. Had she lost her magic again? Did it really not work when she was being controlled by Caleb's touch?

Let me use my magic to stop him, Magda said to her fox. Why don't my spells work?

Your dark magic comes from the Darkness, which is the source of every Shifter's animal energy, replied her fox. *I am your connection to the Darkness, and to the dark magic that comes from it. I control its flow, and I don't want you to use it because I know you will use it to stop him from doing what must happen. Just like you have been stopping it all this while, denying it even though you didn't know you were denying it. This must happen. He is going to claim us, take us, put his seed in us. It is time, and I will not let you stop it.*

"No!" Magda shrieked, pushing at Caleb even as she felt her wetness flow down the insides of her thighs as he rubbed her mound hard, driving his fingers deep into her, pushing the soaked cloth of her gown along with it. "This is a trick! You're under its control just like he is!"

Of course I'm under its control, honey, whispered her fox. *The Darkness is Shifter energy, the energy of the an-*

imal. I am the Darkness, just like your mate's wolf is the
Darkness, just like Adam's dragon, Bart and Bis's bears,
Ash's black leopard. Even Murad's dragon—though that
is an example of what happens when the Darkness takes
over the man too, when the battle for balance is lost.

The battle for balance, Magda thought as she felt
Caleb's hot breath against her cheek as he licked her
neck, his hands beneath her robe, fingers digging
into her ass, driving into her vagina. Balance at every level. The balance between the human and the
animal. The balance within the human itself. And the
balance between two fated mates struggling to find
their way to their destiny.

But what *is* our destiny, Magda thought as she felt
her fox retreat to the background as Caleb pushed
her up against a tree and kissed her hard on the lips
again. She could feel the arousal rip through her body,
but at the same time her mind was still tormented by
that strange promise of a first-born child. The dis-
connect was driving her close to insanity as she felt
the two parts of herself split like they were fighting
each other: The animal that simply wanted its mate;
the human that was holding back as it tried to figure out what was going on, if this was a trap, a trick,
a mistake!

"Our first born child," she groaned as Caleb broke
from the kiss and drew his head back so he could look
at her. His blue eyes were misty with need, but she

could tell that he was fighting with himself just like she was struggling with the needs of the body and the doubts of the mind. He was a soldier, a warrior, a killer, and so he wanted to handle it by drawing his enemy out and facing it on the battlefield. But that wasn't Magda's way. It wasn't the way of the fox. "Our first born child," she said again, touching his face as he looked at her with those hungry blue eyes. "Caleb, we can't. We can't use our child as bait! What kind of parents do that?"

"You don't trust me to take care of you, to take care of my child, my family?" he growled, running the back of his hand along her cheek and tracing his fingers along her neck.

"Of course I do," she whispered. "It's just that I . . . I can't do this until I understand what's going on. Until I get to the bottom of this deal with the Darkness. Caleb, the Darkness isn't some demon or monster. I understand what you're doing, Caleb. I understand that you're a soldier, that you want to face your enemy on the battlefield. But that's a manifestation of your own frustration, your own confusion, your own conflict. We're so close, Caleb. We need to hold on. We're so close!"

"Close to *what*?!" Caleb howled, pressing her neck and then whipping his body back. He spun away from her, his naked body taut and tense, his tattoos shining like they'd been burned fresh onto his skin. "The only thing I'm close to is madness, Magda! We're fated mates! I feel it and you feel it! Our animals know it! What's stopping us from doing what comes naturally?"

"*We* are stopping us!" Magda screamed, her cheeks puffing out as she felt the blood rush to her face. "Why can't you see that? I see it in you. You're holding back too, even though you want to take me, claim me, put your seed in me. You're as unsure about this as I am! You're as fucking *scared* as I am! You just won't admit it!"

Caleb whipped his body back around, his eyes blazing with the darkest blue she'd ever seen. "I don't get *scared*," he whispered, almost spitting the words out. "I don't do fear. Fear is for pussies."

Magda's eyes went black and she shrieked with mocking laughter. "Oh, my God! You are still a child, aren't you? That angry little boy, cowering in the corner, afraid of daddy, powerless to protect mommy!"

With a roar that shook the trees, Caleb was on her, his wolf bursting forth in mid-air, jaws wide open, teeth white as ivory, tongue red as blood. But before the wolf got to her, Magda's fox had come forth, and she bounded out of the way so fast that the wolf went crashing into the tree, almost bringing it down with his strength.

And then Magda the fox was tearing through the woods, a red blur of fox-fur with a gray wolf hot on her heels, both animals wild with pure energy. They crashed through bushes, bounced off gnarled tree-roots, splashed through streams. Rabbits and squirrels stopped to stare. Wild boar tamely sat on their haunches to watch the show. Birds of prey almost fell out of the sky as they got distracted by the streaks of pure energy whizzing through the woods beneath them. Even that solitary German mountain lion emerged from its daytime slumber to shake its head and say, "Diese Amerikaner sind verrückt!" (Translation: These Americans are crazy.)

Magda's snout was hanging open as she raced through the woods, cutting left and right, bounding over obstacles like it was a game. She could feel the wolf's breath hot on her heels, and although she knew the bigger and more powerful wolf would have run her down in a second in an open field, her fox had the advantage in the thick forest with its quickness and ability to change direction on a dime.

"Can't catch me!" Magda squealed as she leapt over a boulder and heard the wolf stumble and roll head over heels with momentum. But the beast kept going, rolling over and landing on its feet, barely losing a step, its breath still hot on Magda's swift paws.

"Oh, I'm gonna catch you, little Red Riding Hood," growled the wolf through its steady panting. "I can run forever. Your tiny legs are going to wear down soon enough. I'm gonna catch you and eat you up, little Red Riding Hood."

"Is that what the big bad wolf does in the story?"

Magda panted as she made a sharp left and barreled down an incline so fast she could barely keep her footing.

"This ain't a fairy tale, little fox," growled the wolf as he crashed down into the shady little valley after her.

"That wasn't much of a fairy tale either, if you think about it," Magda said with glee as she felt the air get cooler as they descended into the valley nestled between the mountains. "Though I always liked the part where the wolf dresses up as the Grandma to trick little Red Riding Hood. In fact, I think I'd like to see you in a grandma-dress. In fact, I think I *will* see you in a grandma-dress!"

She leapt up onto a flat ridge of smooth rock, turning in the air and landing on all fours facing the wolf. Without even realizing she was doing it, she muttered some words and presto, the big bad wolf was suddenly clothed in a polka-dot dress with red frills around the collar!

Magda's trickster fox yipped with delight as the wolf's legs got tangled up in the dress and it fell head-over-heels as it tried to jump up onto the ridge, its snout banging against the base of the ridge, making it roar in surprise. Magda's body was burning with energy, and she just kept yipping out loud as she looked down at her wolf rolling around in a frilly polka-dot dress, its maws wide open as it snorted with laughter.

She had a vague memory of saying something mean to him, something hurtful, something that brought the wolf out in him, brought the Darkness out in him. But now they were laughing, playing, chasing each other like puppies!

And then the wolf stood up on his hind legs, his Change coming through so quick Magda gasped as she saw Caleb the man burst through. The comical dress dropped away as Caleb stood upright and stretched his arms out wide, his body lean and tight, his cock long and hard, his mouth twisted in a half-grin that meant only one thing.

Magda gasped again as she felt her own Change burst through, the woman in her coming forth, naked and ready. She couldn't think anymore. She could barely even see. The energy of her animal was whipping through her, and she didn't give a damn if it was the Darkness taking over, a demon collecting on its deal, or a goddamn fairy godmother that was casting a spell on her.

She felt herself sit down hard on her ass, and then Caleb was standing up against the ridge, pushing her thighs apart as he buried his face between her legs, his tongue driving deep into her vagina and curling upwards, bringing out the animal and the woman in her all at once.

Magda screamed as she came, her climax roaring in like the wind, her eyes going wide and then rolling up in her head as her mate rolled his stiff tongue around her cavern like he wanted to taste every part of her secret space, drink her down, eat her up like the big bad wolf he was.

"You taste so damned sweet, Magda," Caleb growled from between her legs, his tongue still inside her, his voice and lips making her clit shiver as his mouth smothered her mound. "I told you I'm going to eat you up, little Red Riding Hood. Eat you up and then ride you."

Magda's mouth curled into a smile as the ecstasy escalated until her orgasm splintered into a million secondary climaxes. She bucked her hips up into his face, groaned as she felt his stubble prickly and rough against her soft inner thighs, his big hands firmly cupping her ass as he drank her nectar, inhaled her scent, ate her up just like he said he would.

"I don't think that's what happens in that story," she whimpered softly. She fluttered her eyelids as she tried to catch her breath, but then she felt Caleb slide his finger into her rear hole from beneath and she screamed in shock, her eyes flicking wide open, her lips forming a tight circle as she gasped and then moaned out loud. "OK, now *that* certainly doesn't happen to little Red Riding Hood," she managed to say as she slowly lowered her hips onto her mate's middle finger, groaning as she felt it slide deep into her ass in the most filthy, beautiful way.

"This is the adult version," whispered Caleb, his breath hot against her wet mound as he looked up at her, his gaze traveling along her naked body and locking in on her eyes. "The version we'll tell our children."

"Ohmygod, we will *not!*" she squealed as Caleb slowly curled his finger inside her asshole and then gently sucked on her clit again, bringing her so close to another climax that she started to pant and make a gurgling noise like a bubbling brook in the springtime.

But just before that new climax hit, Caleb pulled his face away, flipped her over onto her stomach, and pulled her by the hips until she bent her knees and stuck her ass up in the air. He spread her asscheeks so wide she could feel the air swirling around her opening, and then he let go and brought his open palms down hard on her buttocks, both hands at once, the slaps ringing out like gunshots through the forest.

He spanked her twice, three times, hard and with authority, her cries rippling through the silent forest as her asscheeks shuddered with each strike. Each slap stung like fire, but it felt so damned good Magda couldn't help but arch her back down and stick her ass up in the air as she prepared for the next one. She grinned wide as she realized why she needed to have a "meaty" butt. She was built for her mate. Built for her man. Just exactly right. Like the story of Goldilocks. The adult version, of course.

"That's for making me wear a dress," he whispered,

pressing his face close to her lower back and then slowly running his tongue straight down along her rear crack, leaving a trail of clean saliva. He circled her rear hole with his tongue, licking her carefully and lovingly before driving his tongue inside and holding it there. She could feel his wetness coat her from the inside, and she gasped when he pulled his tongue away and a moment later pressed the massive head of his cock against her tight pucker. "And this," he whispered, his voice a low rumble, "is for imprisoning me in that inhumane, medieval torture device."

Magda felt her breath catch in her throat as she tightened up from behind, her entire body stiffening when she realized what was about to happen. But the head of his cock was already firmly placed at her rear entrance, and Caleb pushed the thick bulb of his erection past her opening so she couldn't close up.

"What are you doing?" she groaned, her eyes wide even though she could barely see. She tried to turn, to move, to do anything, but Caleb's right hand was on the back of her neck, holding her in position as he pulled her left asscheek out with his other hand to give him full access. "What are you doing, Caleb? What are you . . . oh, oh, *oh fuck!*"

Slowly she felt his girth open up her rear canal as he slid his way into her, and now she knew there was no stopping him. This was the need of the animal in him, pure animal, pure beast, pure arousal. Sexual energy in its most dominant form, and she could feel it in herself too as the wetness poured out of her slit like a tap had opened up. For a moment she wondered if they were both animals again, but she could see her boobs hanging down as she hunched her back and looked down. She could see Caleb's heavy balls behind her, full with his seed—seed that he was going to pour into her rear.

And then she understood.

This wasn't the animal in them.

This was the human in them.

Human fear. Human logic. Human reason.

The animals in them wanted to make a baby, but the humans in them were still too scared. Too scared of that strange promise. Still afraid of this thing called the Darkness even though they knew it was a part of them, would *always* be a part of them.

Which meant they were still afraid of themselves in a way. Afraid of what it would mean to accept their fate, accept each other as mates, accept that they were destined not just to be together but to have a child together.

Because what would having a child together mean when I hated being a child and Caleb hated one of his parents, hated himself for being too small, too weak, too young to take control?

She felt her fox move inside her as the thoughts built to a roar in her head, like that bubbling brook was turning into a waterfall. A promise to deliver her first-born to the Darkness? What did that really mean? It had always sounded a bit hokey, a bit like a fairy tale, a bit made-up. The Darkness wasn't going to manifest itself as a monster with ten heads and fifty arms, all its mouths grinning as it snatched her newborn from her breast and ran off giggling into some dark vortex! The Darkness was a necessary part of the universe, a fundamental part of her, a core part of them both. The Darkness *was* her animal, was *both* their animals! So the promise of a newborn as payment was a promise to their own animals, wasn't it?! A promise that the humans in them had been fighting their entire lifes, perhaps without even realizing it!

Magda almost cried as the realization hit her so hard it hurt. The answer had been right there in front of her, straightforward and obvious, clear and concise. But the human in her had twisted it around, made it about some kind of mythical deal with a demon or evil power when it was just her and her animal fighting for control over her identity, her sly fox trying to balance its simple, primal needs with the complicated fears of the woman she was.

A woman who hated her childhood.

Destined to be with a man who hated his father.

"Ohmygod, that's it," she groaned out loud as she felt Caleb begin to pump into her, his grip on her neck tightening as his girth pushed against her inner walls to where she could barely speak. "Caleb, that's it! We're both just afraid of becoming what we hated most, feared most, dreaded most! Deep down I'm terrified of having a child that might have to go through what I went through. And you're terrified of becoming a father! Those are *human* fears, Caleb. The animals in us don't get twisted and turned around because they are all instinct, all primal, the need to reproduce clear and innocent and without prejudice or complication. They've been exasperated for decades as they tried to bring us together, and their needs to have us mate finally brought us back to this place. A place where the animal energy is so strong and raw that we can't deny the need to have a child—a need that's pure and innocent. The deal was with *ourselves*, Caleb! The promise of a first-born is to our own animals! Caleb? Caleb?! *Caleb*?!"

18

Caleb! Caleb! *Caleb*!

The voice came through to him like it was coming from a million miles away, through a tunnel of dark matter, where space and time were rolled up in one, his past and present, his animal and his human, his father and himself.

Am I destined to become my father, Caleb wondered through the haze of arousal as he watched himself slowly enter his mate from behind, his thick, heavy cock parting her smooth rear globes down the middle as she groaned and tightened. She tried to turn her head, but he held her firmly by the neck as he pushed himself all the way deep into her. He didn't want her to look at him. He was afraid of what she'd see: A man who was all wolf, all rage, all disorder and chaos. A man with no control, who hated his woman and hated his child. A man who didn't deserve to have a child, couldn't be trusted with a mate, couldn't trust himself to have a family.

"Caleb!" came her voice again, but he was too far gone to understand what was happening. All he could feel was his teeth biting into his own lips, drawing blood. It tasted sweet, and he pumped his hips as hard as he could, as if his climax was the only goal, raw sex, a release that would end the madness and confusion. Perhaps he'd gone feral. Perhaps he'd gone insane. Perhaps his father's spirit had been haunting him for decades. Perhaps his own wolf had betrayed him. Who the hell knew. Who the hell cared. He just had to finish.

Dark clouds were merging overhead as Caleb gritted his teeth and held his mate down. He'd lost control of himself, and the only thing that felt good was to use his primal strength to control his woman, use his woman, use her for pure carnal pleasure. He leaned his head back and howled in ecstasy as he felt his wolf howl with him. But the animal in him was howling in anguish, like it was in pain, like it was trying to pull him back, pull him out, say something to him.

Forgive him, whispered his wolf from somewhere deep inside. *And forgive yourself.*

"How can I forgive myself for killing my own father?!" Caleb roared as he felt the skies go black over his head, heavy raindrops beginning to fall through the swaying branches.

Not for killing him, replied his wolf. *You didn't kill him—I did. You need to forgive yourself for LOVING him! You need to forgive that angry boy for loving his father even though he hated him. That is the paradox of family, a paradox that only humans have to deal with because of their overdeveloped brains and finely tuned emotions. As an animal I am not burdened with such complex, conflicting emotions. I care about survival and reproduction, and anything that gets in the way must be destroyed. The wolf was my father too, but I killed him without remorse because he threatened our survival. That is the blessing of the Darkness, Caleb. Single-minded purpose. No regrets. Just like an animal feels no remorse when it kills for food or survival or to claim a mate from a rival. Emotions are the battleground of the human, and you have to win that battle if we are to seize our destiny. You understand, Soldier? You want to face the Darkness on the battlefield? Well, you got your wish. YOU are the battlefield. The man in you. I fought for you when the man was just a boy, did what I needed to do for our survival. Now the man needs to fight the battle that the animal cannot fight for him. The battle between conflicting emotions. The war to reconcile love and hate, pain and pleasure, guilt and duty. Understand that pain can bring pleasure. Realize that guilt can go hand in hand with duty. Accept that you can love what you hate.*

And then take our mate.

Seize our fate.

Caleb shouted as the clouds burst open with a thundercrack so loud it almost blew his eardrums out, the dark skies sending pellets of rain down on him like bullets. He pulled out of Magda, groaning from the effort it took to stop himself from coming. His body was shaking, and his mind felt like it had cracked open just like those thunderclouds. He wasn't sure if he was laughing or sobbing, and it was only when he saw Magda turn to him, her face streaked with tears even as she smiled, that he realized he was doing both. It had all rolled into one, he realized as their tears mixed with the rain. Happiness and despair, pain and pleasure, sorrow and delight, guilt and duty, choice and fate, darkness and light, animal and human, man and woman.

"What's happening?" he muttered, blinking as the rain washed over their naked bodies. "What's happening, Magda?"

"Magic," she whispered, wiping his mouth with her hand and looking up at him. With her other hand she slowly gripped his cock, rubbing it back and forth as the rainwater washed it clean. "Magic, fate, and the climax of our story."

"The climax?" he said, grinning as he leaned in and kissed her lips . . . kissed them gently, carefully, with love. Human love. The love of a man for a woman.

"Well, why didn't you say so. Here we go, witch. Here comes your wolf."

And he pulled her hand away and pushed her slowly down onto her back as the rain poured down on them. He gently spread her thighs, fingering her until he felt the thick juices of her feminine wetness flow down his hand as she spread for him. Finally, without hesitation, without doubt, without fear, he pushed himself into her, looking her deep in the eyes as he pressed his hard body down on her soft curves.

"I love you, Magda," he whispered as he felt her warmth envelop him while the cool raindrops bounced off his shoulders and back. "And I'm going to love and protect our children. Our family. The family we were meant to have."

And as she whispered the words back to him, he came. He came like a man, the wolf inside him letting out a low, wailing howl that was a battle cry of victory, letting the universe know that the boy was now a man, a man all the way through, in control of his emotions, in command of his destiny.

A man facing his fate.

An animal claiming its mate.

19

She felt his seed blast into her depths like a volcano but in slow motion, like she could sense every ounce of it flowing through her feminine valley, slow and deliberate even though his power made it hard for her to breathe. She could barely see straight, but somehow she kept her eyes locked on his deep blue gaze as the rain poured down on them like it was washing them clean, washing away their doubts, their fears, erasing the past, heralding the future.

"I love you," she whispered when she heard Caleb say the words, and she felt her fox scream in delight as it experienced the joy of human love, the depth and complexity of the most basic of human emotions, perhaps the foundation of *all* human emotion. "I love you, Caleb. The man and the wolf. All of you."

All of you, she thought as she felt him seize up inside her, flexing his throbbing manhood as she felt the walls of her vagina being forced outwards as he filled all of her with all of him. She spread her thighs wide, bringing her legs up and then clamping them tight around his muscular ass as he drove deeper into her, pushing out more of his hot seed even as she swore she was already overflowing.

They came together for what seemed like hours, and it might have been hours, because when he finally collapsed on top of her, the weight of his body feeling wonderful against her curves, she looked up and saw that the sky was bright blue, the rain was gone, the birds were singing, the animals of the forest out and about as they sniffed the rain-soaked Earth.

Magda stayed in that embrace with her mate, her legs still firmly locked around him, his cock still inside her. She listened to the sounds of the forest, her smile breaking wide when she realized that the animals were welcoming the new arrivals, the fox and its mate, the man and the woman, the witch and the wolf.

"I wish we could just stay here forever," Magda whispered as she felt her fox roll around inside her, a bundle of pure red joy, absolute ecstasy, reveling in the beauty of the moment. It had just been claimed by its mate, and all around them was open forest. It was in fox-heaven! No wonder it wanted to come back here to this place!

"We *are* going to stay here forever," said Caleb without a moment's hesitation. He raised his head, and she could see his wolf alive and alert behind those midnight blue eyes. It had been taking in the sounds and scents of the open forest, listening to the other animals singing their welcome songs, reveling in the feeling of having just claimed its mate out in the wild. It was in heaven too. It didn't want to leave either.

Magda sighed, closing her eyes and trying to push away the thoughts of all that was going on in the world outside. It seemed so far away, like it didn't matter anymore. She felt so peaceful, so complete, so fulfilled that she almost choked.

Perhaps this *is* the end of our story, she thought as she felt her fox yip in agreement. And the beginning of our fairytale. Our happily ever after.

Now you're getting it, honey, whispered her fox. *We have everything we need here. With the wolf by our side, we're the Queen of the Black Forest! His seed is already in us, and he will protect us with his life. We have nothing to fear. Nothing to worry about. Nothing to do but live free like how it's supposed to be! Hunt, mate, and howl with our wolf! Now you're getting it! You can thank me later. Or now. Thank me now, actually.*

Magda giggled as she listened to her fox jabber away like she'd never heard it before. She could tell it was overflowing with excitement, and she closed her eyes and mouthed a silent "Thank You" to her animal. She looked up at Caleb, and immediately she could tell that his wolf was whispering the same thing to him, and it was only then that she felt a strange chill underlying the warm glow that had enveloped them thus far.

"You mean that?" she said softly, not sure if she was scared or delighted. "That we're going to stay here forever?"

"Yes," Caleb said, his jaw tightening, his eyes narrowing. She could see the man in him pushing away the thought that he needed to go back to the real world, take what they'd learned about the Darkness and somehow use it to help his crew fight the battle that was brewing in the outside world. But the wolf in him was clamping down, flatly denying any notion of leaving the safety of the forest. Its seed was in its mate, and now nothing else mattered but the safety of his mate until she gave birth. "The others don't need us. Adam can handle his father the Black Dragon. And John has the entire U.S. military at his disposal. They don't need us. Our children are going to need us, and that's that. This is our home now, Magda. This is where we were meant to be. In the forest, our animals running free, our children growing up with full acceptance of who they are. This is our fate. This is our forever. End of story."

20
<u>ONE YEAR LATER</u>

Is this the end of our story, Caleb wondered as he sat on his haunches, naked and bronzed from the sun, his hair long and wild, a heavy brown beard covering his jawline. He smiled as he watched Magda sitting cross-legged beneath the shade of a moss-covered tree, her breasts full with milk as their seven pups fought for access to her big round nipples.

"Stop it!" Magda yelped as one of the babies pushed its sister away and clamped its sharp little baby-teeth around Mama's nipple and began to suckle like it wanted to drink her dry. "You have to learn to share!

There's enough for everyone, you hear!" She looked up at Caleb, one eyebrow raised, her round face glowing with a mixture of amusement and annoyance. "Are you going to do something or just sit there?"

Caleb sighed, shrugged, and then with a wolfish grin leapt up from the boulder on which he'd been resting his naked ass. A second later he was right there beside his brood, swiftly pulling his seven babies away from Magda's body and sending them tumbling into the soft grass as they giggled and squealed in delight at being manhandled by Daddy.

"If you can't learn to share, then none of you gets any," growled Caleb, sternly looking at his seven pups, three boys and four girls, some with blue eyes, some with brown, all of them a beautiful combination of mother and father, Magda and Caleb, fox and wolf. "Besides, I'm the head of this family, which means I get to drink first."

His cock burst into full hardness as he gathered his mate's heavy breasts in his hands, squeezing so hard she squealed in shock. A moment later his lips were closed tight on her right nipple, and he sucked hard as he felt her warm milk flow into him.

"Stop it, you pervert!" she gasped, grabbing his long hair and yanking his head away from her boob. "Our kids are watching!"

"Good. Then they'll understand that they need to

wait until Daddy gets his fill of Mommy," said Caleb, grinning wide and licking his lips as he felt her sticky milk coat his thick beard. "That's the law of the jungle, rules of the forest, way of the woods."

Magda leaned back on her arms as Caleb massaged her breasts, his arousal growing as he felt her nipples harden while he pinched and pulled at her. She was naked, her dark triangle thick and beautiful as she slowly parted her thighs to reveal her wet slit that looked like a red smile. They hadn't worn clothes for a year now, and already they'd made love a hundred times with the babies around. The separation between human and animal had all but dissolved, and they Changed back and forth at will, almost unconsciously, the fox and the wolf racing through the forest as they hunted, claiming their prey quickly and efficiently, taking just enough for food and nothing more, as was the way of the woods, the rule of life. Emotions like shame and regret weren't even a memory for them, they were so at one with their animals, with the forest, with each other, and Caleb could think of nothing more than satisfying his wolf's basic needs to mate, hunt, and protect its young.

"Speaking of wood," Magda whispered, her eyes shining with arousal as she reached down and gripped her mate's cock firmly around the shaft. Her fingers didn't even go all the way around, he was so thick and swollen, and Caleb arched his neck back and groaned as she gently began to jerk him back and forth. "We should take care of this wood for Daddy Wolf, don't you think?"

"I can't think," Caleb muttered, his eyes rolling up in his head. He licked his lips, the sweet taste of his mate's milk heightening his arousal as he tweaked her nipples and felt her warm cream ooze through his fingers. "I need another drink to clear my head. Come here. Stick your boobs out."

"No!" said Magda, laughing as she pushed his face away, her other hand still firmly grasping his cock. "Save some for your children."

"You dare to defy me?" Caleb whispered, cupping her face with his sticky hands as he drew close. "I'm the King of the Jungle, you know."

"I think a lion might disagree, but all right, Your Majesty. Whatever you say."

Caleb smiled, but a splinter of emotion slithered through him at the mention of the word lion. A hazy image of Darius the Lion Shifter—the beast he'd trained for battle—floated through his mind, and Caleb gritted his teeth as he pushed it away. That was from another world, another time, another place. That wasn't his responsibility. His only responsibility was to his mate, his children, his family. This was his life now. He was free from all that other crap that humans had to deal with. He was all animal. All wolf. All wild.

All . . . darkness?

He felt his wolf stir inside him as he looked into Magda's eyes. She looked so happy, so complete, so at one with her surroundings. This was right, wasn't it? This was their fate, their future, their destiny, wasn't it? How could it be otherwise?

Take her again, whispered his wolf from inside as Magda spread her legs wider, her slit releasing a scent so primal and feminine that Caleb almost came right there and then. *Put your seed in her again. Seven more pups. Seven every year. The forest will be overrun with our offspring.*

Caleb frowned as the arousal swept through him, his mate's scent drawing him closer. She was in heat again, her fox ready to bear more children. He knew it. His wolf knew it. What was there to think about?

Nothing, replied his wolf quickly. *Stop thinking. This is your duty. This is your responsibility. This is your life.*

Caleb blinked as snippets of the life he'd left behind started to break through, disrupting the all-encompassing peace he'd felt over the past year. Indeed, once he'd gotten Magda pregnant, there'd been no doubt in his mind that his only job was to protect her, to raise his children, and to live. Just live. But now . . . now that his pups were here, healthy and happy, Caleb could feel the call of duty, memories of a commitment to his crew, to the world outside his comfy little domain in the woods.

"Magda," he whispered, gently rubbing her rosy

cheeks as they sat naked before each other. "I think
. . . I think . . . I think we have to . . . oh, shit, Magda.
Oh . . . oh, *shit!*"

He howled as Magda bent down in front of him,
her ass sticking up in the air as her face moved down
to his lap. Her mouth was wide open, and a moment
later he felt her lips sliding down over his erect cock,
taking him all the way inside as she opened her throat
for his length. With her other hand she was massaging his heavy balls, coaxing his semen up through his
shaft as all thought dissolved, leaving nothing but
arousal, the need of the animal, the call of the wolf.

He pushed her head down onto his cock, groaning
as she sucked him just the way he liked, going slow
at first and then speeding up until Caleb began to
buck his hips upwards. Then he was up on his knees,
groaning as he watched her magnificent ass spread
as she opened her legs wide to get into a lower position. Soon he was fucking her in the mouth, holding
her by the hair and neck, controlling her as she rolled
her tongue around him.

Is this the Darkness at work, he wondered as he
felt his wolf pant inside him, its energy flooding Caleb with images of life in the forest, just him and his
mate, producing a litter of pups every year, all of
them living happily in the forest like some simplistic
fairy tale. The dream of an animal. The selfish needs
of the beast pushing out the higher needs of the human, the instincts of the animal forcing the human's

sense of duty and responsibility to the background.

Your only duty is to your mate and your pups, snarled his wolf as it licked its chops inside him. *Now stop thinking with your overdeveloped brain. My instincts have led us this far, and all you need to do is trust my instincts. Didn't I save your tiny ass when you were a baby? This is our place now. Our home. We are free here. Free from the troubles of the world. Free from the burdens of civilization. Don't overthink this, Soldier. You've won the battle. This is your reward! A life of peace! Family! Babies! Sex! Hunting! There is nothing else to life!*

"Nothing else to life," Caleb repeated in a trancelike stupor as he watched his mate move back and forth before him. His arousal was spiraling upwards like a typhoon rising from the sea, and he groaned as he felt his animal's energy rise with it. Somewhere inside him he could hear the man he was, the soldier he was, the crewmate he was. But the voice was small, distant, buried beneath the energy of the wolf, the needs of his animal.

"Yes," whispered Magda, pulling her mouth away from him and then turning around and arching her back down. "I'm ready, Caleb. I'm in heat again. I feel it. I'm ready to take your seed again. Seven more pups this year. Oh, Caleb, I'm so happy. I never imagined I could feel this way, living for the moment, nothing but pleasure filling my days, warmth filling my heart! My fox was right. Your wolf was right. The Darkness is part of us. It's who we are. Who we were meant to be! Simple animal energy! Feed, mate, reproduce! It's so obvious when you get down to it, isn't it? The Darkness isn't dark at all! It's just . . . life! It's beautiful! It's . . . it's . . . oh, take me, Caleb. Take me!"

Her words trailed off as Caleb stared down at her spread before him, his open palms coming down hard on her round buttocks, making her squeal in delight. He buried his face between her rear globes, fingering her from beneath as her juices flowed down his hand. He licked her rear hole, dragging his tongue down her crack lengthwise as he felt her reach back between her legs and grasp his cock, pulling him toward her heat, her sex, her feminine. He could feel the draw of her animal, smell the heat of her fox, hear the arousal of the woman in the way she panted for him. She was right. This had to be right. How else could it feel so damned good? This *was* the Garden of Eden, where man and woman lived at one with nature!

Caleb rammed himself into her just as his thoughts exploded into nothing, and Magda screamed as he started to pump immediately, hard and with a manic need to possess her, his fingers digging so deep into her hips that he could see red marks forming on her smooth skin. His balls were swinging back and forth as he grunted with his wolf's need, and he grinned through his shaggy beard as he closed his eyes and silenced the man in him, welcomed the animal, welcomed the Darkness.

21

"**T**he Darkness isn't dark at all! It's light!" Magda heard herself say just as her mate pushed himself into her so deep she swore she could feel him in her throat. Her fox was whipping itself into a frenzy of pleasure inside her, and she smiled wide as she felt her mate's girth stretch her, fill her, claim her afresh.

Now you're getting it, honey, whispered her fox as Magda groaned and gasped from the way Caleb was driving into her from behind. *See how simple it is when you remove all those complications that come from your overdeveloped human brain? All that ambition? That need to 'Change the World'? Hah! Isn't it easier when you just change YOUR world? This is your world now,*

*honey! Trees! Forest! Nature! Your mate! Your pups! Just
like magic! Poof! Done! You have it all now! What more
do you need?!*

"Nothing more," Magda whispered as she felt Caleb's heavy balls slap up against her underside. She
could almost smell his seed, and she panted in antici-
pation of feeling him explode into her depths, flooding her valley, putting seven more pups into her ready
womb. "Poof! Done!"

She could feel her climax rolling in from the distance, and she reached between her legs and grasped
Caleb's balls, massaging them as he slowed his thrusts
down until they were deliberate and deep. She could
hear his heart beat in time with hers, feel his breathing in rhythm with hers, sense his body merging with
hers. It was sublime, like they were one animal, one
being, one creature of single-minded purpose.

But we're not one creature, came the thought from
somewhere deep inside her as her fox's words faded
into the background. Neither of us is. We're animal
but also human. He's a father but also a soldier. I'm
a mother and also a . . . a . . . witch?

Suddenly the memories came rolling back through
her, and Magda's eyes flicked wide open as she remembered why they'd come to this place, why Benson had sent them here, how he'd said they were the
only ones who'd be able to face the Darkness without losing themselves to it. He'd said she was a natural-born witch. A one-of-a-kind Shifter with witch's

blood in her veins. Finding and accepting her mate was one part of the puzzle to understanding who she was. That brought out her fox, her animal, her Shifter self. But there was another part that was still missing, wasn't there?

"My magic," she muttered, realizing that she hadn't used it in over a year. She'd tried a couple of times, but her fox had reminded her that her magic came from the Darkness and the animal controlled the pathway to the Darkness. Her fox had blocked that pathway because it didn't trust the human, and Magda had accepted her fox's words for what they were. But her fox was sly. A trickster. Very capable of saying what it needed to say to get what it wanted. And what did it want?

This, she realized as she felt Caleb flex inside her as he prepared to explode in her depths. This is all it wants. To live here in the forest. To leave behind the complexities of the human world. To just be an animal forever and ever. That's the essence of the Darkness, isn't it? Animal energy. Not evil or demonic energy. Just simple animal energy.

"Except we aren't just simple animals," she groaned as Caleb dug his fingers into her soft flesh and held on. "We're humans too. We're two creatures in one, and we need to balance that. We've spent a year being just animals, mating, feeding, playing with our pups. It's been beautiful and peaceful, pure joy and delight. But slowly we're burying the human parts of ourselves, Caleb. And if we lose touch with our humanity, lose touch with higher level emotions like duty, morality, compassion, then . . . then . . ."

She trailed off as a vision of Murad's Black Dragon came through to her. That was what happened to a Shifter when it lost the human, wasn't it? A Shifter was both human and animal, both dark and light, and its entire existence was a struggle to balance those two parts of itself. But what did balance mean? Did it mean peace and tranquility forever? Dead calm? Equilibrium?

"No," she whispered. "Equilibrium is an illusion. Motion and movement are the foundation of the universe. Back and forth. Up and down. In and out. You can't stop it. Stopping it is death. The Shifter's challenge is to recognize that it is the embodiment of life's energy, that it is doomed to always fight for balance between its animal and its human, its dark and its light. There will never be everlasting peace for a Shifter. That's why the universe blessed us with fated mates! So we don't have to fight that eternal battle alone!"

"Why are you talking so much?" Caleb growled from behind her, pushing into her and holding himself there as he leaned forward. "It's a real buzzkill, Witch."

Magda giggled as she felt his warm breath on her back. She could sense her fox yipping in anger at the delay, and immediately she understood that the human in her was slowly clawing its way back. After a year of the balance swinging towards the animal's need, it was time to satisfy the human's needs.

And those needs were much more than those of the flesh.

They were needs of the soul.

The need to help the world.

The need to fulfill their duty.

The need to be part of a community, a tribe, a bigger family than just them and their pups.

"We need to go back," she said softly, turning her head and looking up at her mate. "It's time, Caleb. If we deny our human needs, we'll become all animal. And then the Darkness might truly turn dark."

Caleb's jaw went tight, and he took a long, slow breath. He was still inside her, but he was holding still, as if his wolf was urging him on even as the man in him was affected by Magda's words.

"What's the use of going back?" he said after a long pause, his blue eyes narrowing as he looked down at her and then slowly began to move inside her again. "You said you've lost access to your dark magic, and without that what use are we to the outside world? If you can't put Murad's dragon back inside him, then we might as well just stay here."

"And what happens to the world?" Magda whispered, feeling her own arousal creeping upwards again. "Who's going to stop the Black Dragon from destroying it all? How long before its fire reaches us here?"

"Adam will have to take care of business," Caleb said with a shrug, even though Magda felt him tense up. "In fact he probably already has. It's been a year, Magda. I don't see any fireballs shooting across the sky. Adam's probably killed his father. Boom. Done. He can handle it. I handled it just fine."

"You didn't kill your father—your wolf did," Magda said softly.

"Same thing," said Caleb stubbornly. "I am my wolf."

"No, the wolf is just a part of who you are, Caleb! Just like the fox is just a part of who I am! This past year has been beautiful as we mated and gave birth and raised our young."

"Exactly," said Caleb. "It's been beautiful, which means it was right."

"Of course it was right! This past year was about accepting each other, indulging our animal selves, repaying the debt that we owe to that part of ourselves. We satisfied the needs of the animal to mate and reproduce. And now it's time to turn our attention back to the needs of the human, the needs of the soul, the needs of the world."

"The world can go fuck itself," Caleb grunted, closing his eyes and slowly beginning to thrust again. "Once I put my seed into you again, you'll forget all this nonsense about the outside world."

The wolf is right, whispered her fox as Magda felt

herself slipping back to that place where pleasure was everything, where things seemed so simple, where she had no duty other than to her mate and pups. *Shut your mouth and spread your legs, honey.*

Magda closed her eyes tight as she felt the conflict brewing inside her, and she opened her mouth in a silent scream of anguish as she tried to reach for her magic. Benson had said she was a natural-born witch, that she had magic that came from the Light. Well, where was it?! Where the hell was it?! It was a lie, wasn't it? She wasn't a natural witch! The only magic came from the Darkness, and it came through her fox! She wasn't a witch! She was just—

"*Ouch!*" came the howl from behind her. "What the hell?!"

Magda gasped as she felt Caleb pull out of her suddenly, and then she frowned when she felt cold metal against her butt. She turned and stared, her mouth hanging open in a mixture of surprise and delight when she saw the metal chastity belt that had begun their courtship back on Caleb, locked tight, padlock swinging, its magical keyhole winking at her.

"But I didn't . . ." she stammered, cocking her head as she tried to understand what the hell had happened. Then she heard a giggle from the bushes followed by a squeal. Two more laughs, another squeal of joy, and finally all seven of their pups were howling and laughing as they crawled into view.

"No way," Caleb said, the anger evaporating as he

stared at his babies and then back at his mate. "Did they just . . . did these critters just . . . no way. No way!"

Magda just blinked absentmindedly as she felt her fox yelp in fury like it had been outfoxed by a bunch of infants. "Oh, God, Caleb! If our kids did that, it means . . . it means that I'm a natural-born witch! Oh, God, Caleb! There's hope! We've got a shot at stopping Murad before Adam has to kill his own father! It's destiny, Caleb! The greater destiny that's part of our fate!"

Caleb slowly began to nod as the steely blue of the soldier in him emerged in his eyes. "Fate," he muttered. "Destiny. More than just the needs of the animal. Which means that meeting and accepting each other wasn't the end of our story. It was the beginning!"

"Now they're getting it," came a deep voice from the woods, and every hair on Magda's head stood up straight as she whipped around and saw two bears standing there, up on their hind legs.

"Better late than never," said the other bear.

Caleb had already Changed to his wolf, and Magda's fox came forth at the same time, the two of them standing in front of their still-giggling pups who were rolling around on the grass like it was all a game.

"Stay back or I'll rip you both down the middle of your big bellies," Caleb growled through his wolf.

"Now turn around and slowly walk away. Walk away, and I promise I won't kill you. Not today, anyway."

"Hear that, love?" said one bear to the other. "He says he won't kill us."

"Huh. Does he know we *can't* be killed?" said the other bear, folding its thick, furry paws across its chest and shaking its big head like it was saying *Tsk Tsk* to the angry wolf.

"Shifters can be killed just fine," Caleb growled, glancing back at Magda before slowly moving toward the bears. "I warned you once. I won't warn you again."

"True. Shifters *can* be killed," said the bigger bear.

"Except we aren't Shifters," said the other bear. "Not anymore, at least. We've already . . . Shifted. See, when a Shifter dies, its animal and human splits. The human goes to the Light. And the animal returns to the Darkness."

"The Light," Magda whispered through her fox. She thought back to what Benson had said about her natural magic—that it came from the Light. Which meant that her magic came from the human side of her, not the animal. Magic that gained power through human emotions like compassion, duty, community.

Her fox slumped its shoulders in defeat as Magda felt the human energy flow through her, felt a different kind of power rise up in her just from the realization that she had that power, that she was born with that power, with that magic, with the duty to use that magic for good.

"So what are you?" Caleb said cautiously, his wolf still in that protective stance, its massive gray body shielding its mate and pups. "Ghosts? Demons?"

"Boo!" said one of the bears with a chuckle.

The other bear snorted with laughter, and then it shook its furry head. "We're soldiers, Caleb. Just like you. But soldiers who fought the wrong enemy. Don't make the mistake we did. Don't let our son and daughter make that mistake."

Caleb frowned, his midnight-blue eyes narrowing as Magda watched. Then the wolf's mouth dropped open, its eyes widening. "Holy shit," he said, taking another step towards the bears and sniffing their scent. "I'd recognize that smell anywhere. You're . . . you're Bart's parents! Mama and Papa to ol' Butterball!"

Magda frowned as her fox sniffed their scent as well, its body tensing up as it recognized them too . . . recognized them not as Bart and Ash's parents, but as the military scientists who'd tried to kill her animal years ago!

"Murderers," Magda whispered, feeling the rage flow through her fox. She could sense it trying to open up a pathway to the Darkness, like it wanted that dark magic back, like it wanted to use the anger and hatred to do something horrible to these two bears. For a moment Magda felt it working, like the fox was harnessing the repressed anger of that girl who'd had her animal stolen from her just when she'd discovered it.

But the two bears just narrowed their brown eyes and stared at her, like they knew exactly what her fox was doing. They knew, and they were . . . they were stopping it! She could feel some power in these two bears blocking her fox from reaching to the Darkness, and Magda blinked as she finally felt the little critter in her give up and yield.

"What are you?" she whispered, not sure if she was relieved or terrified.

"We are exactly what you said," replied one of the bears, its face drooping as it stared mournfully at its mate and then back at Magda.

"Murderers," whispered the other bear. "We spent our lives trying to cure Shifters of what we thought was a disease. We wasted our intelligence, our gift, our potential. It was only when we 'cured' ourselves that we came face to face with the truth."

"And what's the truth?" growled Caleb, still wolf, still wary, still protecting his mate and pups even though Magda could tell he was as curious as she was.

"I think he's interrogating us," said one bear to the other.

"Benson taught him well," grunted the other. "Let's tell him everything before he waterboards us."

The two bears chuckled again, but Magda could sense a deep melancholy in them, a deep sense of regret, guilt, shame. Those were human emotions, the darker side of human emotions, emotions that flow into a human when they forsake the higher emotions of love, compassion, and duty.

"Showing is better than telling," said the first bear, turning and then gesturing with its paw. "Come on, kids. Follow us. All will be revealed in the next book."

"Ohmygod, if this is a cliffhanger, I'm going to—"

"Relax," said Mama Bear with a toothy grin. "When I was pregnant with my kids, I read romance novels all day and night. I know there's nothing that a romance reader hates more than a cliffhanger. Not until they get their happy ending first."

"Are you two married?" said Papa Bear with a raised eyebrow as he glanced at the seven pups crawling around on the grass, tumbling over each other as they giggled and goo-goo'd.

"Just by natural law," said Caleb with a lopsided grin. He glanced almost apologetically at Magda. "We'll make it official when we return to the world."

"About time," said Magda with an amused smile. In an instant she Changed back to human form, looked down at her naked body, and then stuck out her ring finger. "I've been feeling very undressed without a ring."

Everyone laughed, and then Caleb Changed back to the man, joining with his woman as they gathered their seven pups—five in his arms, two in hers—and followed the darkly comical bears into the depths of the forest.

"This better be good," he called after the bears. "Because now even I'm curious. I almost understand why romance readers get so pissed off about cliffhangers."

22

Caleb held his pups tightly in his strong arms as he peered over the cliff. He squinted as he looked down, but all he could see were swirling clouds, dark with rain—or something else.

"What is this place?" he said, frowning as he sniffed the air. But he couldn't pick up any scent. It was strange. Almost impossible. His wolf could smell anything.

"A doorway to the Darkness," said Mama Bear. "A gateway to the place where a Shifter's disembodied animal goes."

"A gateway," repeated Papa Bear as he mournfully

looked down. "And we are the gatekeepers. We denied our true fate, and our fate changed. This is now our fate. To stand at the doorway to a place that we filled by killing so many Shifters' animals."

"I don't understand," Caleb said, finally stepping back from the cliff and turning to Bart's parents. "So you stand here so no one can get in?"

Mama Bear shook her head, smiling sadly as she reached her paw out for her mate's big paw. "No," she whispered. "We stand here so no one can get out. A Shifter's animal without its human is out of balance, lopsided, all Darkness and no Light. We cannot let them out of this place. That is now our responsibility. That is now our forever. This is how we make up for what we've done. It is our responsibility now."

Caleb glanced back at Magda, who was standing a safe distance from the cliff's edge, her two pups clinging tightly to their mother. He could see the determination in her eyes, sense the feeling of responsibility in the way her jaw was set tight. He looked down at the five babies clinging to his arms and body like little monkeys, and he felt his own deeper purpose bubble upwards like a spring coming through rock. His wolf was inside, but it had backed down as if acknowledging that its time had past, that the human was on the upswing again, that the neverending back-and-forth was something that would always be a part of its destiny, that there would be times when the wolf reigned, other times when the man ruled.

Suddenly he could feel the clarity of the soldier rip through him, and then he was thinking hard, the connections forming so fast it almost took his breath away. He thought back to the snippets of information John Benson had fed to them before sending them here: Why had a beast like Hitler emerged from this part of the world? Why had the military set up a Paranormal Research Lab in this place? Why was—

"My school," Magda said, her face twisted into a frown as if she was remembering things from her past too. "It wasn't just a boarding school, was it? It was . . . it was *part* of that secret research lab that Benson talked about!"

Mama Bear quickly glanced at Papa Bear and then nodded slowly. "Yes," she said quietly. "We identified children who showed indications of special abilities, and we brought them here."

"Oh, gimme a break," said Caleb, snorting as he rolled his eyes. "A school for witches? Really?"

"No," said Papa Bear. "Maggie was the only witch. And even her we didn't know about back then. Not until much later."

Magda frowned as she bit her lip. "Special abilities? You mean like psychic powers? Things like that?" She shook her head. "I don't remember any of that. There was no mind-reading going on. I didn't see anyone using telekinetic powers to start a food-fight in the lunchroom."

Mama Bear nodded and sighed. "You're right. The school was a failed experiment. We thought by bringing these supposedly gifted kids together we could develop their abilities to the point where we could . . ."

"Could what?" said Magda. "Counteract the Darkness? Close up the gateway? Create a doorway to the Light that neutralizes the Darkness?"

Papa Bear shrugged. "I . . . I don't know. Something like that. We weren't sure, Magda. None of us were sure. All we know is that it was all a failure. Even the abilities we'd witnessed in the children seemed to go away when we brought them to this place. That wasn't the answer. That wasn't the way to bring balance back to the world. We were searching outside ourselves for an answer, ignoring the truth that the answer lay within us, in who we were, who we were born to be."

"Animal and human in one," said Mama Bear. "We recognized that the Darkness was animal energy, but we mistakenly believed it was evil. We didn't understand that it was just an opposing force to Light—an opposing force that is a necessary part of the universe. By rejecting our animals and killing so many other Shifters' animals, we only tilted the balance further to the Darkness."

"Now you need to tilt it back," whispered Papa Bear,

staring right at Magda. "You're the only one. Witch and Shifter in one. You and your children will slowly help the world regain its balance."

"I . . . I don't know if my natural magic is strong enough," Magda stammered.

Mama Bear sighed and shook her head. "It isn't. Your natural magic will have to coexist with the dark magic that your fox got access to when it ventured to this place all those years ago. You'll have to reclaim that dark magic, control it so it doesn't take over, balance it with the natural magic that comes from the Light."

Magda's face turned ashen as she blinked. "No," she whispered. "You don't understand. The dark magic that flowed through me when I stood by Murad's side was . . . was . . . all-encompassing. Absolute. How can I let that back into me? I have children to think about! I have—"

"You can't do it alone," said Papa Bear. "You can't do it without the support system of the Shifters around you, the bonds of family, the strength of the community. You need your mate, you need his crew, you need the collective."

"And you need it quick," said Mama Bear, turning to the dark clouds swirling in the bottomless valley beneath the cliff. She glanced at Papa Bear, and he turned to face the cliff with her. "Because Murad's

Black Dragon is slowly understanding what it needs to do. Slowly understanding why it's building an army of Shifters."

Caleb felt a chill go through him as he heard a cacophony of noises coming through the clouds beneath them. He looked down, his eyes going wide when he saw flashes of different animals, beasts of every size and shape, mouths open wide, eyes mournful and dead, claws and teeth bared as they tried to leap through the clouds. Already he'd understood that he needed to go back to the world, that defeating the Darkness meant accepting the human in him again, the man in him again, the soldier in him again. And now that soldier had to turn towards his greater destiny, stand side by side with his mate just like his wolf and his man stood side by side within him. He'd faced his own Darkness during that year in the woods, when he was close to deciding to hide from his human needs. He'd faced it and won. Now he needed to save the other Shifters of the world who had to face their own Darkness, fight their own internal battles.

"Only a Shifter can kill another Shifter," Caleb muttered as he connected the dots in his head. "And when a Shifter dies, its animal gets sent to this place, to this dark valley. So every time Murad's Shifter army kills another Shifter, another twisted animal gets sucked into the Darkness. Soon the gates will be broken down, unleashing Shifter-animals without their humans, without balance. Animal energy swarming across the world. Unstoppable Darkness. It's a time-bomb ticking away. A countdown where the number counts down every time the Black Dragon's army sends another Shifter's animal here!"

"The Apocalypse," Magda whispered. "Oh, my God, Caleb! We need to—"

"Go!" rasped Papa Bear, taking his mate's paw as the two of them stepped to the edge of the cliff and prepared to step off into the clouds, to beat back the animals below. "Join with the others before it's too late. Before Adam kills his father, and then you are forced to use your magic on Adam as *he* turns to the Darkness! That will send *all* of you spiraling towards Darkness! A chain reaction which can't be stopped. So go. Please. Go now! *Now!*"

23
ADAM'S LAIR
THE CASPIAN SEA

"**N**ow what?" said Caleb, his face grim as he stared at Benson across Adam's long dining table.

Magda glanced at the solemn faces gathered around the dark teakwood table. The kids were all occupied in the next room, and through the open door she could see her seven infants, so her fox was calm. But the woman in her was peaked with energy, and she could see that every other person in the room was feeling the same. All their animals were calm, relaxed, happy to be around their crewmates, content that their children were safe. The humans, however, were focused, their sense of meaning and purpose sharpened to a fine point. Their animals had found their fated mates, and that was all they cared about. But a human's sense of destiny and fate ran deeper, and the separation between the simple needs of the animal and the complex needs of the human was never more clear to Magda.

She smiled at the other women in the room—Bis and Ash. She sighed as she surveyed the serious expressions on Bart and Adam's faces. Then she took a breath as she listened to Benson speak.

"There's no sign of the Black Dragon," he said slowly, his gray eyes steady and unblinking. "He's gone off the radar. Three months of raiding, rampaging, and burning. Then poof, he was gone. No sign of his Shifter army either. It's like they've been disbanded. Turned into sleeper agents. All gone underground, waiting for the Black Dragon to re-emerge and call them to arms."

"That doesn't make sense," Bart the Bear said, rubbing his square jaw and frowning. "A dragon that's lost to the Darkness doesn't just stop its rampage out of the blue."

"Unless it is beginning to understand what it can do with that Darkness," said Magda. She looked at Bart and then at Ash before scanning the roomful of

Shifters and one CIA man. "That's what your parents told us, Bart. The Black Dragon is starting to understand that no matter how powerful it is, it can't keep rampaging until it destroys the world. Even it needs reinforcements to do that. So it's realizing that instead of just running wild and killing everything, it needs to kill only Shifters. After the initial explosion of pent-up energy, it's calmed down a bit. Become more calculating."

"And more dangerous," said Benson softly.

"So you're saying it's on the hunt for Shifters to kill now? Just Shifters?" said Bart, now scratching his head. "But there aren't that many of us, right, John? It took you years just to scrape up the three of us!"

Benson nodded, his face in a deep frown. "It's not easy to find a Shifter. Most of your kind are living in denial, a state of dormancy. It's only when they wake up to their true selves that they show up on the map."

"Wait, you have a map that lights up with a dot every time a Shifter wakes up?" said Bart, his eyes opening wide like a child watching a cartoon.

Benson groaned and rubbed his forehead. "Not now, Bart. Real questions only, please."

"Shifters can sense when there's another Shifter in the area," said Adam quietly, half-smiling at the big Butterball Bart. "That's why Murad disbanded his army, spread out his troops, sent them back into human society like drones searching for something.

They'll be able to find other Shifters. Kill them. Send their animals to the Darkness, building up its power until Bart and Ash's parents can't hold them back anymore."

"Which takes me back to my original question," said Caleb impatiently. "Now what? What do we do?"

"We do what my parents said," Bart snapped, his own impatience seeming to rise. "We find Murad and send in your witch. Poof. Put the genie back in the bottle! End of story."

"I'm not sending the mother of my children to face a Black Dragon on the warpath!" growled Caleb, his hairs standing on end. He glanced at Adam, his jaw tight. "We're soldiers, aren't we? We'll find him and we'll . . ."

He didn't finish the sentence, and Magda understood that Caleb couldn't ask Adam to kill his own father even though the thought must certainly have crossed Adam's mind that he might have to do it. At the same time, Magda wasn't confident enough that she knew how her dark magic and natural magic would combine to once again control Murad's dragon now that it had been unleashed. Caleb was right—she was a mother. Yes, the human in her was responding to the call of what she believed was her higher purpose. But she couldn't ignore the needs of her fox to protect its pups. She *needed* her fox. She needed *all* of them.

"We can't find Murad if he's all Darkness, if he's not really a Shifter anymore," said Magda. "But we can find the others in his Shifter army. Pick them off one by one."

Caleb frowned as he turned to her. "What? Find the Shifters I trained and then . . . *kill* them? What are you saying, babe?"

"I didn't say kill them," Magda replied with a smile. She looked at Benson. "I meant convert them. Bring them over to our side. Bring their animals and humans in balance."

"How?" said Caleb. "I know those beasts, Magda. Darius the Lion. Everett the Tiger. Hell, those are wild animals! Close to feral! Who knows what state they're in by now! You want them to join our crew? How?"

"The same way this crew got back together," said Magda firmly. "The same way I was brought into this crew. The same way Bis and Ash were brought in. Fate."

"Fated mates," said Bis, nodding her head slowly as a smile formed on her dark red lips. "Help them connect with their fated mates, and they'll find their balance."

Ash nodded earnestly, leaning forward on the table, her heavy breasts pushing up against the edge. "That's how we pick them off," she said, her eyes wide with delight. "As each Shifter finds his mate, it will understand what it means to find balance, how it can be both animal and human at once, darkness and light at once."

"Exactly!" said Magda, feeling her energy matching up perfectly with these curvy women who already felt like friends, like sisters, like . . . family. "And as we get each of Murad's Shifters matched up, his army will get smaller. Eventually the Black Dragon will be forced to come out of hiding as it seeks out Shifters to kill. That'll give me time to work on my magic, to understand what your parents said about accepting my dark magic along with my natural witchcraft."

"Perfect!" Bis squealed, clapping her hands. "We'll be Shifter Matchmakers! We should have a name for it! What should we call ourselves?"

"SSA," said Caleb with a grin.

Bart cocked his head and glanced at his buddy. "That's the name for that bogus agency you made up to recruit Shifters to Murad's army! What was it called?"

"The Shifting Sands Agency," said Caleb. "But let's just condense it to SSA." He glanced down at Magda's thighs that were full and heavy as she sat on her chair. Then he looked at the other two big, beautiful women mated to his buddies. "Spell that backwards, Butterball. Slowly."

Bart frowned. "A. S. S." he said slowly. "Ass? Ass. *Ass!*"

He roared with laughter as he got it, thumping the

table so hard all the plates and silverware jumped three feet into the air. All the women turned bright red, but by then they were all laughing. Soon even the stoic CIA-man Benson was in on it, and before long the tension had dissolved to a feeling of pure optimism, a sense that they were on the right path, that even though their animals had found their happy endings, the real story was just beginning.

"Just one thing missing," said Bart suddenly, his gaze resting on Magda's ringless fingers. "Hold on. I'll be right back."

He pushed his chair back from the table, and a moment later Changed to bear form and barreled out of the room so fast everyone just stared in amused wonder.

"Where the hell is *he* going?" said Adam with a frown. Then his face turned red with anger and he leapt up from his chair and headed towards the stairs just as an unholy crash shook the castle's foundations. "Oh, hell no! My vaults! My *vaults!*"

But Adam was knocked back on his heels as Bart the Bear came bounding back up the stairs, a massive diamond ring in his front paw. Adam roared again, wisps of smoke pouring from his nostrils as Magda sensed his dragon's hoarding instincts come into effect.

"Simmer down, hothead," Bart growled at his Alpha. "Just giving you an excuse to pile up some more trinkets in your treasure chest." A moment later he knocked Caleb off his chair with one swipe of his massive paw. "On your knees, brother. Do I gotta show you how it's done? All right." He turned to Magda as she giggled. "Dear Miss Witch. On behalf of my shy-ass brother the Flying Squirrel and my stingy-ass Alpha the Big Bird, I present you with this diamond ring and cordially ask you to—"

"Give me that, you dumb furball," Caleb barked, snatching the ring from the oafish bear. He shook his head and rose up on one knee, looking deep into Magda's eyes. Then his smile was gone as his lips trembled as if he'd understood that this was important, that a natural law union between two animals was fine and good, but the humans in them needed to make it official. The human woman needed her proposal, her wedding, her happily ever after.

"Yes," she whispered as the room went silent and Caleb whispered the question. "Of course I will. I'm yours, Caleb. I always was. Your woman. Your mate. Your witch."

Your witch.

In darkness and in light.

In animal and in human.

Always and forever.

The witch and the wolf.

∞

EPILOGUE

"So we have a name, a mission, and a plan," said Benson to the group gathered around the table. "But where do we begin? The CIA has a lot of lists, but we don't have a list of Shifters. For once I'm at a loss. I don't know how to actually find any of these Shifters from Murad's disbanded army!"

Caleb cleared his throat as he scanned the memories of the Shifters he'd managed to recruit. Almost all of them had come to him through those ads. He had no idea where they'd come from—not really.

But then he thought back to something Darius the Lion Shifter had mentioned in passing when they'd been shooting the shit after fighting in the sandy desert training ground.

"Training you beasts is like herding cats," Caleb had complained as he examined two big scratches on his thigh from the lion's jaws.

"Hah," Darius had quipped, raising an eyebrow at the other Shifters. "Nice one. But I actually did herd cats, you know. I was pretty damned good at it too."

"What?" Caleb had said. "You were a cat-wrangler?"

Darius's gold eyes had narrowed, his mane thick and full as it glowed beneath the desert sun. "Something like that. Back then I was the King, you know. The goddamn King." A low growl had emerged from his thick throat. "King of the Ring, they called me. King of the Ring."

"King of the Ring," Caleb muttered as he thought back to that conversation with Darius the Lion. "Holy shit! I know where we can find the Lion!"

"Where?!" said everyone else almost in unison.

Caleb snickered as he shook his head. "Get ready, folks. I'm going to introduce you to the King of the Ring."

"King of the Ring?" said Bart. "What ring?"

"The big ring. Trapeze, clowns, jugglers, and . . . animals," said Caleb. "Pack up the kids, everyone. We got a family vacation coming up."

"Where?" said Bart, still frowning even as everyone else seemed to slowly get it.

"The circus, Butterball," said Caleb with a grin.

"We're going to the circus?" said Bart, his

face lighting up like he was one of the kids. "The goddamn *circus*?"

"Yup," said Caleb. "Where else are you going to find a lion tamer?"

∞

FROM THE AUTHOR

You guys ready for some old-fashioned Shifter match-making? Then get TAMED FOR THE LION and read on as our core crew tries to save the world, one Shifter couple at a time!

By now you know what to expect from the Curves for ShiftersSeries: Drama, Madness, and over-the-top Steam. A happy ending for every couple in every book, but also an overarching story that's going to keep building!

And if you're all caught up with this series, why don't you try my CURVES FOR SHEIKHS books? They've got everything that makes an Annabelle Winters novel what it is:
Twists and turns.
Darkness and Light.
Always and Forever.

Love,
Anna.

PS: Sign up for my private list at annabellwinters.com/ join to get five sizzling bonus scenes from my Sheikhs series!

∞